Noah's Child

ERIC-EMMANUEL SCHMITT

Translated from the French by
Adriana Hunter

Atlantic Books
London

First published in France as *L'Enfant de Noé* by Éditions
Albin Michel, S. A., 2004

First published in Great Britain in 2012 by Atlantic Books,
an imprint of Atlantic Books Ltd
This paperback edition published in Great Britain in 2013
by Atlantic Books

Liberté · Égalité · Fraternité
RÉPUBLIQUE FRANÇAISE

This book is supported by the French Ministry of Foreign Affairs, as part of
the Burgess programme run by the Cultural Department of the French
embassy in London. (www.frenchbooknews.com)

1 2 3 4 5 6 7 8 9

A CIP catalogue record for this book is available from the British Library.

Paperback ISBN: 978-1-84887-419-0

Printed and bound by CPI Group (UK) Ltd, Croydon, CR0 4YY

Atlantic Books
An imprint of Atlantic Books Ltd
Ormond House
26–27 Boswell Street
London
WC1N 3JZ

www.atlantic-books.co.uk

For my friend Pierre Perelmuter,
whose story, partly,
inspired this book

———————

In memory of Abbé André,
curate of the parish of Saint-Jean-Baptiste
in Namur,
and of all the Righteous among the Nations

One

When I was ten years old I was among a group of children put up for auction every Sunday.

We weren't sold: we were asked to file across a stage in the hopes of finding a taker. Our own parents, finally back from war, could have been in the audience, or perhaps a couple who wanted to adopt us.

Every Sunday I stepped on to the boards, hoping I would be recognized or, failing that, chosen.

Every Sunday, in that covered courtyard at the Villa Jaune, I had ten paces in which to show myself, ten paces in which to secure a family, ten paces to stop being an orphan. The first few steps were no trouble, I was propelled on to that stage by my impatience, but I flagged halfway across, and my calves laboured painfully to cover the last metre. The far end was like the edge of a diving board, with only emptiness beyond. An abyss of silence. Somewhere in those rows of heads, those hats and partings and chignons, a voice was meant to cry 'My son!' or 'He's the one! He's the one I want! I'll adopt him!' Clenching my toes and straining my whole body in anticipation of this cry which would save me from abandonment, I double-checked that I looked my best.

I had been up since dawn, leaping from the dormitory to the cold basins where I scoured my skin with a bar of rock-hard green soap that was slow to soften and miserly with its lather. I had already straightened my hair a dozen times to ensure it did as it was told. My Sunday-best blue suit was now too narrow at the shoulders and too short in the arm and the leg so I huddled inside the rough fabric to disguise the fact that I had grown.

We found it hard to tell whether the waiting beforehand was a pleasure or torture; preparing ourselves to make a leap without knowing what sort of landing lay ahead. Maybe we would die a death? Maybe we would be cheered?

Of course, my shoes didn't help. Two bits of mushy cardboard, with more holes than substance. Great gaps tied over with raffia. A well-ventilated design, open to the cold and the wind and even to my own toes, these boots only resisted the rain now that they were encrusted with several layers of filth; I couldn't take the risk of cleaning them for fear they would fall apart. The only indication that my shoes actually were shoes was the fact I wore them on my feet. If I had held them in my hand I can guarantee people would have kindly shown me to the bin. Perhaps I should have stuck to the clogs I wore during the week? Mind you, the visitors to the Villa Jaune wouldn't be able to see them from down below the stage. And even if they could, surely I wasn't going to be turned down for a pair of shoes! Hadn't Léonard the carrot-top found his parents even though he filed past barefoot?

'You can go back to the refectory, my little Joseph.'

Every Sunday my hopes died with those words. Father Pons gently implied that, yet again, today wasn't the day, and I had to leave the stage.

About turn. Ten paces and you disappear. Ten paces and you're back to the pain. Ten paces and you're an orphan again. The next child was already hovering at the other end of the stage. My ribs crushed in on my heart.

'Do you think I can do it, Father?'

'Do what, my boy?'

'Find some parents.'

'*Some* parents! I hope *your* parents have escaped danger and will turn up soon.'

I exhibited myself without success so often I ended up feeling it was my fault. Actually, they were the ones taking too long to come. To come back. But could they really help it? Were they still alive?

The war had now been over for some weeks, and the time for any hopes and illusions had come to an end along with it. Those of us left, the hidden children, had to face reality and find out – with a brutality that felt like a blow to the head – whether we were still part of a family or were alone in the world.

I was ten years old. Three years earlier my parents had entrusted me to strangers.

Two

It all started in a tram.

Maman and I were travelling across Brussels, sitting at the back of a yellow carriage that spat sparks as the tram trundled on with its metallic roar. I thought it was the sparks from the roof that made us go faster. I was on my mother's lap, wrapped in her sweet smell, snuggled against her fox-fur collar, speeding through that grey city. I was only seven years old but I was king of the world. Step aside! Make way! Cars parted, horses panicked, pedestrians fled as the driver transported my mother and me like royalty.

Don't ask me what my mother looked like: how do you describe the sun? Maman radiated warmth, strength and joy. I remember the effect she had rather than her features. When I was with her I could laugh, and nothing terrible could ever happen to me.

So when some German soldiers got on I wasn't worried. I just pretended to have lost my tongue because I had an agreement with my parents: they were afraid Yiddish would give me away so, as soon as a grey-green uniform or a leather coat came near, I didn't speak a word. By then, in 1942, we were supposed to wear yellow stars but my father, skilled tailor that he was, had found a way of making our coats so we could tuck away the star and produce it when necessary. My mother called them our 'shooting stars': there one moment, gone the next.

While the men chatted, paying no attention to us, I could feel my mother tensing and shaking. Was it instinctive? Did she hear some telltale sentence?

She stood up, put her hand to my mouth and, at the next stop, bundled me down the steps.

Out on the pavement, I asked, 'But we're not home yet! Why've we stopped here?'

'We're going for a bit of a stroll, Joseph. All right?'

Well, I wanted whatever my mother wanted, even though I struggled to keep up with her on my seven-year-old legs, because she was suddenly walking so much more quickly and sharply than usual.

On the way she suggested, 'We're going to go and see a really big lady, would you like that?'

'Yes. Who?'

'The Comtesse de Sully.'

'Is she as fat as the butcher's wife?'

'What ever made you say that, Joseph?' she scolded.

'Well, you said she was really big . . .'

'Oh,' she smiled, 'I meant she was a noblewoman.'

'A what?'

While she explained that somebody noble was of high birth, descended from a very old family and commanded a great deal of respect simply because of their nobility, she led me to a magnificent private residence and took me into the hall where we were greeted by servants.

I was disappointed, however, because the woman who came over to us wasn't at all what I had imagined; although she came from an 'old' family, the Comtesse de Sully looked very young, and despite being a 'big' lady of 'high' birth, she was hardly taller than I was.

They spoke quickly and quietly, then my mother kissed me and asked me to wait there until she came back.

The small, young, disappointing Comtesse took me to her drawing room where she offered me tea and cakes, and played the piano for me. Given the height of the ceilings, the generosity of the tea and the sheer beauty of the music, I was prepared to reconsider my assessment and, sinking comfortably into a luxurious armchair, I conceded that she was after all a 'big lady'.

She stopped playing, looked at the clock with a sigh and came over to me, her forehead furrowed by some concern.

'Joseph, I don't know whether you'll understand what I'm going to tell you but, by family tradition, I cannot hide the truth from a child.'

This might be a custom for the nobility, but why was she making me a part of it? Did she think that I was noble? Was I, actually? Me, noble? Maybe . . . Why not? If, like her, it meant not being big or old, then I was in with a chance.

'Joseph, you and your parents are in serious danger. Your mother heard some people saying there were going to be arrests in your neighbourhood. She's gone to warn your father and as many friends as she can. She's left you here with me, so that you're safe. I hope she'll come back. Yes, I really hope she comes back.'

Well, I would rather not be noble every day: the truth hurt.

'Maman always comes back. Why wouldn't she?'

'She might be arrested by the police.'

'What's she done?'

'She hasn't done anything. She's . . .' The Comtesse heaved a long plaintive sigh that made her pearls clink softly. Her eyes filled with tears.

'She's what?' I asked.

'She's a Jew.'

''Course she is. We're all Jews in my family. Me too, you know.'

And because I was right she kissed me on both cheeks.

'What about you, are you a Jew?' I asked.

'No. I'm Belgian.'

'Like me.'

'Yes, like you. And I'm a Christian,' she added.

'Is Christian the opposite of Jew?'

'The opposite of Jew is Nazi.'

'Don't they arrest Christians?'

'No.'

'So is it better to be Christian?'

'It depends. Come on, Joseph, I'll show you round the house while we wait for your mother to come back.'

'There! You see, she *will* come back!'

9

The Comtesse de Sully took my hand and led me up the staircases that soared up through the floors, and I gazed at vases and paintings and suits of armour. In her bedroom I found an entire wall filled with dresses on hangers. We were surrounded by clothes and thread and fabric at home in Schaerbeek too.

'Are you a tailor like Papa?'

She laughed.

'No. I buy the clothes that people like your daddy make. They have to work for someone, don't they?'

I nodded but didn't tell the Comtesse that she can't have chosen her clothes from us because I had never seen such beautiful things in Papa's workshop, the embroidered velvets and lustrous silks, the lace cuffs and buttons that glittered like jewels.

The Comte came home and, when the Comtesse had explained the situation to him, he took a good look at me.

Now, he was much more how I pictured a nobleman: tall, thin, old – at least, his moustache made him look venerable. He eyed me from such a great height that I realized the ceilings must have been raised for his sake.

'Come and have supper with us, my child.'

He had a nobleman's voice, I was sure of that! A thick, solid, deep voice, the same colour as the candlelit bronze statues around us.

During the meal I politely carried on with the obligatory conversation even though I was still consumed by the whole question of class. Was I noble, or not? If the de Sullys were prepared to help me and take me into their home, was it because I was in some way related to them? And therefore noble?

When we moved through to the drawing room to drink orange-blossom tea, I could have voiced my questions out loud but, for fear of a negative answer, I felt happier living with the flattering possibility a little longer . . .

I must have fallen asleep before the doorbell rang. Stiff from lying in an armchair, I looked up to see my parents appearing on the landing from the hall, and that was when I first understood that they were different. Their shoulders were bowed beneath their drab clothes, they were carrying cardboard suitcases, and spoke hesitantly, anxiously, as if they feared the dazzling hosts now facing them as much as the darkness they had just left behind. I wondered whether my parents were poor.

'It's a round-up! They're arresting everyone. Even

11

women and children. The Rosenbergs. The Meyers. The Laegers. The Perelmuters. Everyone . . .'

My father was in tears. Given that he never cried, I was embarrassed to see him break down in front of people like the de Sullys. What could this over-familiarity mean? That we were noble? I didn't move from my chair because they thought I was asleep, but I watched and listened to everything.

'Leave? But where would we go? To reach Spain we'd have to cut across France and that's no safer than here. And, without false papers, we'll . . .'

'You see, Mischke,' my mother said, 'we should have gone to Brazil with Aunt Rita.'

'When my father was already ill? Never!'

'He's dead now, God rest his soul.'

'Yes, it's too late.'

Comte Sully brought a note of calm into the conversation.

'I'll take care of you,' he said.

'No, Monsieur le Comte, it doesn't matter what happens to *us*. It's Joseph who needs saving. Him first. And him alone, that's the way it has to be.'

'Yes,' agreed my mother, 'Joseph's the one who needs to go somewhere safe.'

If you asked me, being singled out like this

confirmed my hunch: I was definitely noble. At least in my family's eyes.

The Comte reassured them again.

'Of course I'll take care of Joseph. And I'll take care of you too. However, you'll have to agree to being temporarily separated from him.'

'My Josephshi . . .'

My mother collapsed into the arms of the little Comtesse who patted her shoulders soothingly. My father's tears may have embarrassed me, but my mother's devastated me.

If I was noble I couldn't go on pretending to sleep! I leaped chivalrously from my chair to comfort her. Only, I don't know what came over me once I reached her because the exact opposite happened: I clung to her legs and started sobbing even more loudly than she. In just one evening the de Sullys had seen the whole family cry! After a display like that, it would be tough getting anyone to believe we were nobility.

My father then provided a diversion by opening his suitcases. 'Here, Monsieur le Comte. I'll never be able to pay you so I'll give you everything I have. These are my last suits.' And he picked up a succession of hangers with the jackets, trousers and waistcoats he had made. He smoothed each piece with the back of his hand, a gesture he often made in his shop, a swift stroking action that showed off the merchandise by emphasizing the supple drape of the fabric.

I was relieved my father hadn't been into the Comtesse's bedroom with me and had been spared the sight of her beautiful clothes, otherwise he would have dropped dead on the spot, racked with shame for daring to present such everyday things to such refined people.

'I don't want any kind of payment, my friend,' said the Comte.

'I insist . . .'

'Don't humiliate me. I'm not doing this for personal gain. Please, keep your precious treasures, you might need them.'

The Comte had called my father's suits 'treasures'! I was missing something. Could I have been wrong?

We were taken up to the top floor of the house and given a room under the eaves.

I was fascinated by the field of stars revealed by the window cut out of the roof. Until then I had never had the chance to watch the sky because all I could see through the small window of our basement apartment were shoes, dogs and shopping bags. To me, the vaulted universe, that deep dark velvet dotted with stars, seemed the logical conclusion to a nobleman's home where beauty leaped out on every floor. It made sense that the de Sullys didn't have six households and all their offspring overhead, but the sky and the stars which weigh nothing. I liked being noble.

'Joseph, you see that star there?' my mother said. 'That's our star. Yours and mine.'

'What's it called?'

'People call it the evening star; but we'll call it "Joseph and Maman's star".'

My mother had a way of renaming stars.

She put her hands over my eyes, twirled me round then pointed at the sky.

'Where is it? Can you point it out to me?'

I learned to recognize 'Joseph and Maman's star' without fail in all that vastness.

My mother hugged me to her and sung a Yiddish lullaby. As soon as she finished the song she asked me to point to our star. Then she sang again. I fought off the urge to slide into sleep, eager to live this shared moment in all its intensity.

My father was at the far end of the room, bent over his suitcases, folding and re-folding his suits and grumbling to himself. In between two murmured couplets from my mother I managed to ask him, 'Daddy, will you teach me to sew?'

Slightly thrown, he didn't answer straight away.

'Please,' I insisted. 'I'd like to make treasures, like you.'

He came over to me, and this man who was frequently so stiff and withdrawn held me to him and kissed me.

'I'll teach you everything I know, Joseph. And even what I don't know.'

His coarse, prickly black beard must usually have hurt him because he often rubbed his cheeks, and wouldn't let anyone touch it. That evening it can't have been troubling him and he allowed me to finger it inquisitively.

'It's soft, isn't it?' whispered my mother, blushing, as if confiding in me.

'Come on, don't talk nonsense,' he scolded.

Even though there were two beds, one double and one single, Maman insisted I slept with them in the double bed. My father didn't object for long. He had really changed now that we were noble.

And there, gazing at the stars that sang in Yiddish, I fell asleep in my mother's arms for the last time.

Three

We never said goodbye to each other. Perhaps it was because everything happened in such a muddle. Or maybe it was deliberate on their part. They probably couldn't face such a scene, much less subject me to it . . . the thread was broken without my even realizing it: they went out the following afternoon and never came back.

Every time I asked the Comte and the tiny Comtesse where my parents were, the answer invariably came back: 'Somewhere safe.'

I made do with that because all my energy was taken up discovering my new life: my life as a nobleman.

When I wasn't on my own exploring every nook and cranny of the house, or watching the maids in their constant dance of polishing silver, beating carpets and plumping up cushions, I spent hours in

17

the drawing room with the Comtesse who worked on improving my French, and wouldn't allow me to utter a single expression in Yiddish. I was all the more compliant with her because she spoiled me with cakes and piano waltzes. Apart from anything else, I was convinced that I would achieve true noble status only by mastering this language Sadly, it struck me as lacklustre, difficult to pronounce and nothing like as amusing and colourful as my own, but it was gentle, measured and distinguished.

In front of visitors I had to call the Comte and Comtesse 'Uncle' and 'Aunt' because they were passing me off as one of their Dutch nephews.

I had reached the point where I believed it myself, when the police surrounded the house one morning.

'Police! Open up! Police!'

Men thudded violently on the front door; the bell wasn't enough for them.

'Police! Open up! Police!'

The Comtesse, wearing only a silk negligee, burst into my room, grabbed me in her arms and took me to her bed.

'Don't be afraid of anything, Joseph, answer in French, just like me.'

As the police climbed the stairs, she started reading

a story, the two of us propped up against the pillows as if this was all quite normal.

When they came in they glowered at us furiously.

'You're hiding a Jewish family!'

'Search wherever you like,' she said haughtily, 'put a stethoscope to the walls, break open trunks, turn over all the beds: you won't find anything. On the other hand, I can guarantee you will be hearing from me first thing tomorrow morning.'

'Someone has come forward with information, Madame.'

Still keeping her composure, the Comtesse showed her indignation that they would believe anyone at the drop of a hat. She warned that this would not stop here, it would go all the way to the palace because she was a close friend of the Queen's, then she announced that this blunder would cost these little civil servants their jobs – oh yes, they could take her word on that!

'Now, do your searches! And get on with it!'

Confronted with so much confidence and indignation, the officer in charge almost took a step back.

'May I ask you who this child is, Madame?'

'My nephew. His father is General von Grebels. Do I need to show you a family tree? You're trying to commit career suicide, my man!'

After a fruitless search, the officers left feeling awkward and ashamed, and mumbling their apologies.

The Comtesse leaped out of bed. Her nerves at breaking point, she started laughing and crying at the same time.

'There, you've found out one of my secrets, Joseph, one of my womanly tricks.'

'What's that?'

'Making accusations instead of giving explanations. Attacking when under suspicion. Lashing out rather than going on the defensive.'

'Is it just for women?'

'No, you can use it too.'

The following day the de Sullys told me I could not stay with them any longer because their lie would not stand up to investigation.

'Father Pons is going to come and he'll take care of you. You couldn't be in better hands. You should call him "Father".'

'Yes, Uncle.'

'You won't call him Father so that people think he's your father, like calling me Uncle. His name is Pierre Pons but everyone calls him Father.'

'Even you?'

'Even us. He's a priest. We call him Father when we speak to him. So do the German soldiers. Everyone does. Even people who don't believe.'

'People who don't believe he's their father?'

'Even people who don't believe in God.'

I was very impressed at the thought of meeting someone who was 'Father' to the whole world, or was taken to be. He must be very important, anyway, because I'd heard that name Pons before: the Comtesse had introduced me to something she called *pierre ponce**, which sounded just the same. It was a soft light piece of grey stone that she gave me when I was in the bath, and told me to rub my feet with it to remove toughened dead skin. This mouse-shaped thing fascinated me because it could float (not something you would expect of a stone) and changed colour as soon as it was wet (going from greyish white to coal black).

'So is there some connection between Father Pons and *pierre ponce*?' I asked.

The de Sullys burst out laughing.

'I don't see what's so funny,' I said, put out. 'He could have discovered it . . . or invented it. I mean, someone had to!'

_____
* Pumice stone

21

No longer laughing at me, the de Sullys nodded their heads.

'You're right, Joseph: it could have been him. But there's actually no connection between them.'

Still, when Father Pons rang the doorbell and came into the de Sullys' house I knew straight away it was him.

This tall, narrow man looked as if he was made up of two separate parts that were completely unrelated: his head and the rest of him. His body seemed weightless, a length of fabric with no contours, a black robe so flat it could have been on a hanger, and peeping from beneath it were shiny boots that didn't seem to be attached to ankles. But his head sprang out at you: chubby, pink, lively, fresh and innocent, like a baby after a bath. You felt like kissing it and taking it in your hands.

'Good afternoon, Father,' said the Comte. 'This is Joseph.'

I scrutinized him, trying to understand why his face didn't really surprise me but also was a sort of confirmation. A confirmation of what? His dark, dark eyes looked at me kindly from behind the light-framed, round lenses of his glasses.

Then it suddenly dawned on me.

'You haven't got any hair!' I exclaimed.

He smiled and in that moment I started to like him.

'I've lost a lot and I shave what little I have left.'

'Why?'

'To save time on brushing it.'

I laughed out loud. So he himself wasn't sure why he was bald? It was too silly . . . The de Sullys were looking at me quizzically. Didn't they know either? Did I have to tell them? But it was so obvious: Father Pierre Pons's head was as smooth as a pebble because he had to match his own name – *pierre ponce!*

They were still looking baffled so I sensed that I should be quiet. Even if it did make me look stupid . . .

'Can you ride a bike, Joseph?'

'No.'

I didn't dare admit the reason for this failing: since the beginning of the war my cautious parents had stopped me playing in the street. I was therefore a long way behind children my age in all sorts of games.

'Well, I'll teach you,' said the priest. 'You try to stay on behind me. Hold on tight.'

23

And there in the de Sullys' courtyard, struggling to be worthy of their pride, it took me several attempts to stay on the luggage rack.

'Let's try out in the street now.'

When I managed it, the Comte and Comtesse came over and kissed me hurriedly.

'See you soon, Joseph. We'll come and visit you. Watch out for Big Jack, Father.'

I hardly had time to grasp that this was goodbye before the priest and I were wheeling through the streets of Brussels. As all my attention was focused on keeping my balance, I couldn't give in to my sadness.

With thin rain transforming the tarmac into a slick mirror-like surface, we sped onwards, quivering and wobbling on the bike's narrow tyres.

'If we come across Big Jack, lean against me and we'll chat to each other as if we've known each other for years.'

'Who's Big Jack, Father?'

'A Jewish traitor who goes round in a Gestapo car. He points out the Jews he recognizes for the Germans so they can arrest them.'

As it happened, I'd noticed a slow-moving black car following us. I glanced behind me and, through the windscreen, sitting between two men in dark coats, I spotted a pasty sweaty face scouring the pavements of Avenue Louise with beady eyes.

'Father, it's Big Jack!'

'Quick, tell me a story. You must know some jokes, Joseph, don't you?'

Without even picking out the best ones, I started churning out my stock of jokes. I would never have guessed Father Pons would find them so funny. He roared with laughter. Intoxicated with this success, I started giggling too, and by the time the car sidled right up to us I was already too full of myself to notice.

Big Jack stared at us sulkily, patting his flabby cheeks with a small folded white handkerchief. Then, disgusted by our jollity, he told the driver to drive on.

Shortly after that Father Pons turned down a side street, and the car disappeared from sight. I wanted to carry on with my career as a comedian but Father Pons exclaimed,

'Stop, Joseph, please! You're making me laugh so much I can't pedal properly.'

'Too bad: you won't get to hear the one about the three rabbis trying out a motorbike . . .'

*

At nightfall we were still travelling. We had left the city far behind and were cutting through the countryside where the trees were darkening to black.

Father Pons wasn't tiring but he hardly spoke, settling for the odd 'OK?', 'Are you holding out?' and 'Not too tired, Joseph?' Still, the further we went the more I felt we knew each other, probably because my arms were round his waist, my head was resting against his back and I could feel the warmth of his thin body gently seeping through the thick fabric of his robe. At last there was a sign saying Chemlay, Father Pons's village, and he braked. The bike gave a sort of whinny and I fell into the ditch.

'Well done, Joseph, you pedalled well! Thirty-five kilometres! For a first time, that's incredible!'

I got back up, not daring to contradict the priest. In fact, to my great shame, I hadn't pedalled on our journey, I had let my legs dangle. Were there pedals I hadn't even noticed?

He put the bike down before I had time to see, and took me by the hand. We cut across a field to the first house on the outskirts of Chemlay, a low, squat building. Once there, he gestured to me to keep quiet, avoided the front door and knocked at the door to the cellar.

A face appeared.

'Come in quickly.'

'This is Mademoiselle Marcelle, our pharmacist,' whispered Father Pons, leading me in.

Mademoiselle Marcelle hastily closed the door and took us down the few steps that led to her cellar, lit by a measly oil lamp.

Children found Mademoiselle Marcelle frightening, and when she leaned towards me she lost none of her impact: I almost cried out in disgust. Was it the shadows? The way she was lit from below? Mademoiselle Marcelle looked like all sorts of things, but not a woman; more like a potato on the body of a bird. Her heavy, misshapen features, wrinkled eyelids and dark, dull, rough uneven skin made her face look like some root vegetable harrowed over by a farmer: jabs of his pick had marked out a thin mouth and a couple of small bulges for her eyes, while a few sparse hairs – white at the root and reddish at the ends – suggested the thing might sprout again in the spring. Perched on thin legs, bent forward, with a large stomach which bulged outwards from her neck down to her hips, like a plump red robin, hands on hips and elbows back as if ready to take flight, she peered at me, preparing to peck.

'A Jew, of course?' she asked.

'Yes,' said Father Pons.

'What's your name?'

'Joseph.'

'Good. No need to change the name: it's Christian as well as Jewish. And your parents?'

'Maman is Léa and Papa's Michaël.'

'I want to know their surname.'

'Bernstein.'

'Oh, that's a disaster! Bernstein . . . We'll say Bertin. I'll get some papers for you in the name Joseph Bertin. Here, come with me for the photograph.'

In a corner of the room a stool was waiting for me, in front of a painted background of woods and sky.

Father Pons tidied my hair, straightened my clothes and asked me to look at the camera, a large wooden box with concertina sides, on a framework almost as tall as a man.

Just then a flash of light leaped around the room, so bright and disconcerting I thought I had dreamed it.

While I rubbed my eyes, Mademoiselle Marcelle slipped another plate into the accordion, and the strange lighting phenomenon happened again.

'Is there more?' I asked.

'No, two should be enough. I'll develop them overnight. You haven't got fleas, I hope? Anyway, you'll have to put this lotion on. Or scabies? Well, I'll give you a good scrub, and rub you down with sulphur. What else? A few days, Monsieur Pons, and I'll get him back to you, is that all right with you?'

'That's all right with me.'

It wasn't all right with me, not at all: I was horrified at the thought of staying alone with her. Not daring to admit this, instead I asked, 'Why did you say *monsieur*? You're supposed to say Father.'

'I say what I like. Monsieur Pons knows perfectly well I hate priests. I had quite enough of churches and priests foisted on me as a child and now I'm sick if you try and give me the host. I'm a pharmacist, the first female pharmacist in Belgium! The first woman to qualify! I've done my studies and I know about science. So let other people keep their 'Father'! Besides, Monsieur Pons doesn't hold it against me.'

'No,' said the priest, 'I know you're a good person.'

She started muttering as if the word 'good' had too much of a churchy whiff about it.

'I'm not good, I'm fair. I don't like priests, I don't like Jews, I don't like Germans, but I can't bear to see anyone harm children.'

'I know you love children.'

'No, I don't love children either. But they *are* human beings.'

'Well, then you love the human race!'

'Oh, Monsieur Pons, stop wanting me to love something! That's typical of a priest, that sort of thing. I don't love anything or anyone. My job is being a pharmacist, which means helping people stay alive. I do my job, and that's all there is to it. Come on, out, clear off! I'll get this boy back to you all sorted out, nice and clean and tidy, with papers that mean he'll be left in peace, damn it!'

She turned on her heel to avoid further conversation. Father Pons leaned towards me and gave me a secret smile.

'"Dammit" has become her nickname in the village. She swears more than her father who was a colonel.'

Dammit brought me some food, put up a bed for me and, in a voice that tolerated no disobedience, ordered me to get some rest. As I fell asleep that evening, I couldn't help feeling a certain admiration for a woman who said 'Damn it' so naturally.

*

30

I spent several days with the intimidating Mademoiselle Marcelle. Every evening, after a day's work in her dispensary above the cellar, she would toil away in front of me, unashamedly making my false papers.

'Do you mind if I say you're six instead of seven?'

'I'm nearly eight,' I protested.

'Well, you're six then. It's safer. We don't know how long this war will go on. The longer it is before you're a grown-up the better off you'll be.'

When Mademoiselle Marcelle asked a question there was no point in answering because she was only ever asking herself, and only expected her own replies.

'We'll also say your parents are dead. They died naturally. Let's see, what sort of illness could have taken them?'

'A tummy pain?'

'Influenza! A virulent strain of influenza. Tell me your story, then.'

When it came to their repeating what she had invented, Mademoiselle Marcelle suddenly did listen to other people.

'My name is Joseph Bertin, I'm six years old, I was born in Anvers and my parents died of influenza last winter.'

'Good. Here, have a mint pastille.'

When I pleased her she behaved like a lion tamer, tossing me a treat that I had to catch in mid-air.

Father Pons came to see us every day, and did nothing to disguise how hard he was finding it to root out a home for me.

'All the "safe" local farming people have taken in a child or two already. On top of that, any possible candidates are hesitating, their hearts would go out more readily to a baby. Joseph's quite big now, he's seven.'

'I'm six, Father!' I exclaimed.

To congratulate me for that contribution, Mademoiselle Marcelle popped a sweet in my mouth and said grimly to Father Pons, 'If you like, Monsieur Pons, I could threaten the hesitators.'

'What with?'

'Damn it, no more medicine if they won't take in our refugees! They can turn up their toes and die!'

'No, Mademoiselle Marcelle, people have to agree to take this risk of their own free will. They could be sent to prison for colluding . . .'

Mademoiselle Marcelle spun round towards me.

'How would you like to be a boarder at Father Pons's school?'

Knowing there was no point in replying, I didn't even move but let her carry on.

'Take him to the Villa Jaune with you, Monsieur Pons, even if that *is* the first place they would come looking for hidden children. But, damn it, with the papers I've made for him . . .'

'How will I feed him? I can't ask the authorities for any more extra ration tickets. You know the children at the Villa Jaune are underfed as it is.'

'Hmm, that's not a problem! The burgomaster's coming here for his injection this evening. I'll take care of him.'

After dark, when she had wound down the metal shutter outside her dispensary (making as much noise as blowing up a tank), Mademoiselle Marcelle came down to the cellar to get me.

'I might well need you, Joseph. Could you come upstairs and stay in the coat cupboard without breathing a word?'

She was annoyed when I didn't give her an answer.

'I asked you a question, damn it! Are you stupid or what?'

'Yes, that's fine.'

When the doorbell rang, I slipped in between the heavy hanging fabrics with their smell of mothballs, while Mademoiselle Marcelle took the burgomaster through to the room at the back. She took his raincoat and rammed it against my nose.

'I'm finding it more and more difficult getting hold of insulin, Monsieur Van der Mersch.'

'Yes, times are hard . . .'

'To be honest, I won't be able to give you your injection next week. Shortages! Hold-ups! It's all finished!'

'My God . . . my diabetes . . .'

'There's nothing I can do, Sir. Unless . . .'

'Unless what, Mademoiselle Marcelle? Tell me! I'll do anything.'

'Unless you give me some ration tickets. I could exchange them to get your medicine.'

'That's impossible,' the burgomaster replied in a panicky voice, 'I'm being watched . . . the local population has grown far too much in the last few weeks . . . and you know exactly why . . . I can't ask for any more without attracting the attention of the Gestapo . . . it . . . it would have repercussions for us . . . for us all!'

'Take this piece of cotton wool and press firmly. Harder than that!'

While she gave her curt instructions to the burgomaster, she came over towards me and whispered quickly and quietly between the cupboard doors, 'Take his keys from his coat, the ones on the metal ring not the leather one.'

I wasn't sure I had heard her correctly. Did she sense that? She added between gritted teeth, 'And get a move on, damn it!'

She went back to finish the burgomaster's bandage while I fumbled in the dark to relieve him of his keys.

Then, after her visitor had left, she let me out of the cupboard, sent me down to the cellar and set off into the night.

Very early the following morning Father Pons came to bring us the news:

'Action stations, Mademoiselle Marcelle, someone's stolen the ration tickets from the town hall!'

She rubbed her hands together.

'Really? How did they manage that?'

'The looters forced the shutters open and broke a window.'

'Goodness! Has the burgomaster been damaging his own buildings?'

'What do you mean? That he stole . . .?'

'No, I did. With his keys. But when I put them back in his letterbox this morning I felt sure he would fake a break-in so no one would suspect him. Here you are, Monsieur Pons, have this book of ration tickets. It's yours.'

Although she was surly and incapable of smiling, Mademoiselle Marcelle's eyes gleamed with delight.

She pushed me by the shoulders.

'Go on! Off you go with Father Pons now!'

By the time my bag had been packed, my false papers gathered together, and the story of my invented life rehearsed again, it was lunchtime when I reached the school.

The Villa Jaune was like a giant cat nestled on the top of the hill. The stone paws of the front steps lead up to its mouth, a hallway once painted pink, and weary-looking sofas could pass for a dubious tongue. On the first floor two large bay windows, shaped like oval eyes, dominated the front of the building and stared down at what was going on in the courtyard, between the gate and the plane trees. Up on the roof, two dormer balconies bristling with cast iron were reminiscent of ears, and the refectory building curled round like a tail to the left-hand side.

There was nothing to explain why the place was known as the Villa Jaune, the Yellow Villa. A century of filth, rain, wear and children bouncing balls against the render had mottled and striped the cat's fur so it was now more a dull tawny colour.

'Welcome to the Villa Jaune, Joseph,' said Father Pons. 'From now on it will be your school and your home. There are three sorts of pupil: day boys who go home for lunch, day-boarders who stay for lunch, and boarders who live here. You'll be a boarder: I'll show you your bed and cupboard in the dormitory.'

I mused on those unfamiliar distinctions: day boys, day-boarders and boarders. I liked the fact that there wasn't just an order but a hierarchy: from the summary pupil to the complete student, via half students. So I was going straight into the top class. Deprived of noble status in the last few days, I was happy to be granted this alternative distinction.

In the dormitory the whole business of seeing my cupboard went right to my head – I'd never had a cupboard of my own before. I gazed at its empty shelves and dreamed of all the treasures I would arrange on them, not really taking into account the fact that, for now, I had only two used tram tickets to put there.

'Now I'm going to introduce you to your godfather. All boarders at the Villa Jaune are protected by one of the big boys. Rudy!'

Father Pons cried 'Rudy' several times without success. Prefects relayed the name in an echo. Then the other pupils. Eventually, after what seemed to me an unbearably long time and with the whole school turned upside-down, the boy by the name of Rudy appeared.

When he promised me a 'big' boy as a godfather Father Pons really meant it: Rudy went on for ever. He reached such a height he seemed to be hanging by a wire from the back of his shoulders: his arms and legs dangled in mid-air and his head wobbled, lolling forward heavily, weighed down by hair that looked too dark, too thick and too straight – apparently amazed to be there at all. He came over slowly, as if apologizing for his gigantic size, like a dinosaur casually saying, 'Don't worry, I'm very friendly, I only eat grass.'

'Yes, Father?' he said in a deep but muted voice.

'Rudy, this is Joseph, your godson.'

'Oh no, Father, that's not a good idea.'

'It's not open to discussion.'

'He looks a nice boy . . .' Rudy mumbled. 'He doesn't deserve this.'

'I'm asking you to show him round the school and teach him the rules.'

'Me?'

'With all the punishments you've had, I think you know them better than anyone else. When the second bell goes you can take your godson to the younger boys' classroom.'

Father Pons slipped away. Rudy looked at me like a pile of logs he had to carry on his back, and heaved a sigh.

'What's your name?'

'Joseph Bertin. I'm six. I was born in Anvers and my parents died of Spanish 'flu.'

He looked up at the ceiling in exasperation.

'Don't recite the whole thing – wait till you're asked the questions if you want people to believe you.'

Annoyed by my blunder, I put the Comtesse de Sully's advice into practice and went straight on to the attack: 'Why don't you want to be my godfather?'

'Because I'm a liability. If there's a pebble in the lentils, it'll be on my plate. If a chair's going to break, it'll be the one I'm sitting on. If a plane falls out of the sky, it'll land on me. I'm bad luck for me and bad luck for anyone else. The day I was born my father lost his job and my mother started crying. If you give me a plant to look after, it dies. If you lend me a bike, that'll die too. I'm the kiss of death. When the stars look at me they shiver. And the moon hides behind a cloud. I'm an all-round disaster, a mistake, a catastrophe, bad luck on two legs, a real *schlemazel*.'

The more misery he piled on – with his voice ricocheting from deep to squeaky because of all the emotion – the more hysterically I laughed. In the end I asked, 'Are there any Jews here?'

He stiffened. 'Jews? At the Villa Jaune! None! Ever! Why do you ask?'

He grabbed me by the shoulders and stared at me.

'Are you a Jew, Joseph?'

He peered at me harshly. I knew he was testing my composure. Beneath his severe expression there was a plea: 'Lie well, please, give me a wonderful lie.'

'No, I'm not a Jew.'

He released his grip, reassured.

'Anyway,' I went on, 'I don't even know what a Jew is.'

'Neither do I.'

'What do Jews look like, Rudy?'

'Hook nose, bulbous eyes, heavy jowls, sticky-out ears.'

'Apparently, they even have hooves instead of feet, and a tail.'

'Have to look into that,' said Rudy, apparently seriously. 'Mind you, at the moment Jews are mainly hunted down and arrested. Just as well you're not one, Joseph.'

'And it's just as well you're not one, Rudy. But you should still avoid speaking Yiddish and saying *schlemazel* instead of unlucky.'

He winced. I smiled. We had each discovered the other's secret; we were in it together from now on. To seal our agreement, he made me carry out a complicated routine with my fingers, palms and elbows, then spit on the ground.

'Come and have a look round the Villa Jaune.'

Quite naturally he took my small hand in his big hot paw, as if we had always been brothers, and introduced me to the world in which I would spend the years to come.

'But still,' he muttered between his teeth, 'I do look like a victim, don't you think?'

'If you learned to use a comb, it would change everything.'

'But look at me! Have you seen what I look like? I've got feet like meat plates and great mitts for hands.'

'That's because they've grown before the rest of you, Rudy.'

'I'm expanding, getting bigger! Just my luck to turn into a target!'

'If you're tall you make people feel safe,' I suggested.

'Really?'

'And you get the girls.'

'Really . . . still, you have to be a hell of a *schlemazel* to call yourself a *schlemazel*!'

'It's not good luck you need, Rudy, it's a brain!'

And that was how our friendship began: I took my godfather under my wing from the start.

On the first Sunday, Father Pons summoned me to his office at nine o'clock in the morning.

'Joseph, I'm very sorry but I'd like you to go to Mass with the other boarders.'

'All right. Why are you sorry?'

'Doesn't it upset you? You'll be going to a church, not a synagogue.'

I explained that my parents didn't go to a synagogue, and that I suspected they didn't even believe in God.

'It doesn't really matter,' Father Pons concluded. 'You can believe in what you like, the Jewish God, the God of the Christians or nothing at all, but here you need to behave like everyone else. We're going down to the church in the village.'

'Not the chapel at the end of the garden?'

'It's no longer in use, deconsecrated. Anyway, I want the people in the village to know all of my flock.'

I ran back to the dormitory to get ready. Why was I so excited about going to Mass? I probably felt there was a great advantage in becoming a Roman Catholic: it would protect me. Better, it would make me normal. Being Jewish meant my own parents couldn't bring me up, my name was better off being replaced, and I constantly had to lie and control my emotions. So what was in it for me? I was very keen to become a little Catholic orphan.

We walked down to Chemlay in our blue cotton suits, in two files in descending order of height, stepping to the rhythm of a scout song. Outside each house we were greeted with kindly eyes, people smiled and gave us a friendly wave. We were part of what made Sunday special: Father Pons's orphans.

Only Mademoiselle Marcelle, standing on the

43

front step of her pharmacy, looked about ready to bite. When our priest, who was bringing up the rear, passed her she couldn't help herself grumbling, 'Going off to have their heads filled with rubbish! Go on, feed them on smoke! Give them a dose of opium! You think it's good for them but drugs are poisonous – specially religion!'

'Good morning, Mademoiselle Marcelle,' replied Father Pons with a smile. 'You're at your loveliest when you're angry, as every Sunday.'

Surprised by the compliment, she retreated furiously to her shop, pulling the door closed so quickly she almost broke the bell.

Our group trundled through the church porch with its disturbing sculptures, and then I saw the inside of a church for the first time.

Rudy had warned me that I had to dip my fingers in the font, make the sign of a cross over my chest, then perform a swift genuflection as I set off down the aisle. Led by those in front of me and jostled by those behind, I watched in terror as my turn drew closer. I was frightened that when I touched the holy water a voice full of rage would ring out round the walls, crying: 'That child isn't Christian! Get him out! He's a Jew!' Instead, the water quivered as I touched it, clung to my hand and ran, fresh and pure, along my fingers. Feeling encouraged, I concentrated on marking out a perfectly symmetrical cross over my torso, then flexed one knee in the same place my friends had, before going over to join them in our pew.

'We are gathered here in the house of God,' began a shrill voice. 'Thank you, Lord, for allowing us into your house.'

I looked up: as houses go, it was quite a house! Not just anyone's house! One with no doors or internal walls, with coloured windows that didn't open, pillars that had no function at all, and arched ceilings. Why were the ceilings curved? And so high? And why weren't there any lights hanging from them? And why had someone lit candles all round the priest when it was broad daylight? With a quick glance round I checked there were enough seats for all of us. But where was God going to sit? And why did all these people huddled on the stone floor of this house take up so little room? What was the point of all that space around us? Which bit of his house did God live in?

The walls started to vibrate and this rumbling became music: the organ was playing. The high notes tickled my ears and the low ones reverberated through my buttocks. The melody spread lushly, expansively through the building.

In a flash I understood perfectly: God was there. All around us and above us. He was the air quivering and singing with music, he was the air bouncing off the arches, the air pressing up into the dome. He was the air bathed in light from the coloured windows, the air that glowed and shimmered and smelt of myrrh, beeswax and lily nectar.

My heart was brimming and felt strong. I took great deep breaths of God, almost to the point of fainting.

The liturgy went on around me. I didn't understand any of it but watched the ceremony with lazy fascination. When I made an effort to identify the words, their meaning was beyond my intellectual grasp. God was one person, then two – the Father and the Son – and sometimes three – the Father, the Son and the Holy Spirit. Who was the Holy Spirit? A cousin? Sudden panic: there were four of him now! The parish priest of Chemlay had just added a woman, the Virgin Mary. Confused by the rapid multiplication of Gods, I gave up on this game of Happy Families and threw myself into the songs because I liked a good sing.

When the priest talked about handing out little round biscuits, I was about to join the queue but my friends held me back.

'You're not allowed to. You're too young. You haven't been confirmed.'

Although I was disappointed, I gave a sigh of relief: they hadn't stopped me because I was a Jew so it obviously didn't show.

When we got back to the Villa Jaune I ran to find Rudy and share my excitement with him. I had never been to the theatre or to a concert so I associated this Catholic celebration with the thrill of a performance. Rudy listened kindly then nodded his head.

'But you haven't seen the best of it . . .'

'What's that?'

He got up to take something from his cupboard and waved at me to follow him into the grounds. Sheltered from prying eyes under a chestnut tree, we sat cross-legged on the ground and he showed me what he was carrying.

It was a missal, bound in unbelievably soft leather, its pages edged in gold that seemed to refer back to the gold treasures on the altar, with silk bookmarks that reminded me of the priest's green robes. He opened it and took out some beautiful cards, all bearing pictures of a woman: it was always the same woman although her features, her headdress and the colour of her eyes and hair varied. How could you tell it was the same person? From the glow of her forehead, her clear-eyed expression, her incredibly pale skin with a dusting of pink on the cheeks, the simplicity of her long, draped gown and her presence – dignified, dazzling, majestic.

'Who is she?'

'The Virgin Mary. The mother of Jesus. The wife of God.'

There was no doubt about it, she definitely had that divine essence. She was radiant. And it was contagious; even the card seemed less like cardboard than meringue, as brilliant white as whipped egg whites, and it was embossed with designs that gave a lacy quality to those delicate blues and ethereal pinks, pastel colours softer than clouds in the first tickle of dawn.

'Do you think it's gold?'

'Of course.'

I ran my finger over and over the precious-looking crown around that peaceful face. I was touching gold, stroking Mary's headdress. And the mother of God was allowing me to do it.

Without warning, my eyes filled with tears and I let myself slide to the ground. Rudy did too. We cried softly, holding our communion cards to our hearts. We were each thinking of our own mother. Where was she? Was she as serene as the Virgin Mary at that moment? Was her face lit up with the love that had leaned over us a thousand times and that we recognized in these cards, or was it twisted with sorrow, fear or despair?

I started singing my mother's lullaby quietly to myself, gazing up at the sky through the branches. Rudy's hoarse voice joined mine, two octaves below me. That was how Father Pons found us, two children singing a Yiddish rhyme and crying over naïve images of the Virgin Mary.

Sensing the man's presence, Rudy fled. At fifteen he was even more afraid of being ridiculed than I was. Father Pons came and sat down beside me.

'You're not too unhappy here, are you?'

'No, Father.'

I gulped back my tears, wanting to please him.

'I really enjoyed Mass,' I said. 'And I'll be happy to go to catechism this week.'

'That's good,' he said without much conviction.

'I think when I'm bigger I'll be a Catholic.'

He looked at me kindly.

'You're Jewish, Joseph. Even if you choose my religion, you'll still be Jewish.'

'What does being Jewish mean?'

'That you were chosen. You're descended from the people chosen by God thousands of years ago.'

'Why did he choose us?' I asked. 'Because we were better than the others? Or worse?'

'Neither. You don't have any particular assets or faults. It just happened to be you, that's all.'

'What just happened to be us?'

'Having a mission. A duty. To bear witness before all men that there is only one true God, and, through that God, to make men respect their fellow men.'

'I don't think we've done a good job, have we?'

Father Pons didn't answer.

'We were chosen all right,' I went on, 'but as targets. Hitler wants us dead.'

'But that could be why, don't you think? Because you are an obstacle to his barbarities. It's the mission God gave you that is unique, not you yourselves. Did you know Hitler also wants to get rid of Christians?'

'He can't. There are too many of you!'

'For now, he can't. He tried in Austria and very quickly gave up. Still, it's part of his plan. Jews first, then Christians. He's starting with you. He'll finish with us.'

I realized that there was a feeling of solidarity behind what Father Pons was saying, not just kindness. It reassured me a little. Then I remembered the Comte and Comtesse de Sully.

'Father? If I'm descended from this line that's gone on for thousands of years, and it's respectable and everything, does that make me noble?'

'Yes,' he said, after a surprised pause, 'of course you're noble.'

'That's what I thought.'

I was relieved to have my intuition confirmed.

'To me, all men are noble.'

I ignored this addition and focused only on what suited me.

Before leaving, Father Pons patted me on the shoulder.

'This might shock you,' he said, 'but I don't want you taking too much interest in the catechism or Catholic worship. Just settle for the minimum, all right?'

He walked away, leaving me seething: so, because I was a Jew, I wasn't really allowed to be part of the normal world! I was just being lent a tiny corner of it.

I couldn't grab it for myself! The Catholics wanted to stick together, bunch of hypocrites and liars!

I was furious and went to find Rudy so that I could blurt out my anger towards Father Pons. He didn't try to calm me down but encouraged me to keep my distance.

'You're right not to trust him. That oddball's not everything he seems. I've found out that he's got a secret.'

'What secret?'

'Another life. A hidden life. And one he's ashamed of, I'll bet.'

'What is it?'

'No, I mustn't say anything.'

I had to pester Rudy all afternoon until eventually, exhausted, he told me what he had discovered.

Every night after lights out, when the dormitories were closed, Father Pons crept silently down the stairs, unlocked the back door as carefully as a thief, went out into the school grounds and didn't come back for as much as two or three hours. While he was out he left a light on in his apartment to give the impression he was there.

Rudy had noticed and then checked these comings and goings when he himself was nipping out of the dormitory to go and smoke in the toilets.

'Where does he go?' I asked.

'I haven't a clue. We're not allowed out of the Villa.'

'I'm going to follow him.'

'You! You're only six!'

'Seven, actually. Nearly eight.'

'You'd get expelled!'

'Do you really think they'd send me back to my family?'

Even though Rudy refused point-blank to be my accomplice, I did manage to persuade him to give me his watch, and I waited impatiently for nightfall, not even having to fight off the urge to sleep.

At half past nine I snaked between the beds out on to the corridor and from there, hidden by the large stove, I watched Father Pons go down the stairs and sidle silently along the walls like a shadow.

With devilish speed he undid the chunky lock on the back door and slipped outside. Slowed by the full minute it took me to close the door without any creaking, I almost lost track of his slight figure disappearing through the trees. Was this really the same man, the worthy priest who saved children, now scurrying away under a clouded moon, more sinuous than a wolf as he skirted round bushes and stumps that tripped me up as I followed barefoot without my clogs? I trembled at the thought of being left behind. Worse than that, I was afraid he might vanish because he seemed such an evil creature that night, implicated in all sorts of strange spells.

He slowed down in the clearing at the far end of the grounds. The boundary wall rose up behind him. There was only one way out, the low iron door that opened on to the road, next to the deconsecrated chapel. For me the chase ended there: I would never dare carry on, in pyjamas and with freezing bare feet, tailing him through that unfamiliar countryside in the dark. But he went up to the small church, took a disproportionately large key from his cassock, opened the door and snapped it shut behind him, locking it.

So was this Father Pons's secret? He went to pray alone at night, on the quiet, at the bottom of the garden? I was disappointed. Was that it? How humdrum! My toes were wet and I was shivering with cold but all I could do now was go back.

All of a sudden the rusty door swung open and an

intruder, someone from outside carrying a bag over his back, came into the grounds. Without a moment's hesitation, he went over to the chapel and knocked on the door in a quiet rhythmical way, probably conforming to some code.

Father Pons opened the door, exchanged a few whispered words with the stranger, took the bag then locked himself in again. The man left straight away.

I stayed behind my tree trunk, open-mouthed with amazement. What sort of trafficking was Father Pons involved in? What was he collecting from that bag? I sat down on some moss, resting against an oak tree, determined to wait for the next delivery.

The nocturnal silence crackled all around me, as if burning with a fire of tension. Furtive sputtering sounds, cracks followed by nothing and explained by nothing, brief rustlings and cries that were as incomprehensible as the mute terror they provoked in me. My heart was beating too fast. A vice was crushing my skull. My fear was producing all the symptoms of a fever.

There was only one thing I found reassuring: the tick-ticking of Rudy's watch. It was there on my wrist, friendly and unflappable, not in the least awed by the shadowy darkness, still telling the time.

At midnight Father Pons came out of the chapel, locked it up carefully and headed back to the Villa.

I was so exhausted I almost stopped him in his tracks then and there, but he slipped between the trees so quickly that I didn't have time.

On the way back I was less cautious than on my outward journey. I crushed several twigs underfoot. With each crunch, Father Pons stopped anxiously and peered into the darkness. When he reached the Villa Jaune, he went inside and I heard the scrape of keys as he locked up.

Finding myself locked out of the boarding house – now, that was something I hadn't thought of! The building stood before me, upright, compact, dark and hostile. The cold and the hours of waiting had drained my strength. What was I going to do? Not only would everyone discover, come morning, that I'd spent the night outside, but where was I going to sleep now? Would I even still be alive in the morning?

A hand came down on to my shoulder.

'Come on, get inside quickly!'

I jumped automatically. Rudy eyed me up and down with a pitying expression.

'When I didn't see you come up after Father Pons I realized you had a problem.'

Even though he was my godfather *and* was unbelievably tall *and* I had to make his life difficult if I wanted to maintain my authority . . . I threw myself into his arms and – for the time it took to shed a few tears – accepted that I was seven years old.

In break time the following day I told Rudy what I had discovered. With a knowing nod, he pronounced his diagnosis:

'Black market! Like everyone else, he's trading on the black market. That's all it is.'

'What's he getting in that bag?'

'Well, food of course!'

'Why doesn't he bring the bag back here then?'

Rudy floundered at this obstacle.

'And why does he spend a couple of hours in the chapel without any lights on?' I went on. 'What's he doing?'

Rudy ran his fingers through his thick hair as if trying to pluck an answer from it.

'I don't know, do I? . . . Maybe he eats what's in the bag!'

'Father Pons eats for two hours and he's still that thin? And everything in that huge bag? Do you really think so?'

'No.'

During the day I watched Father Pons at every opportunity. What mystery was he hiding? He was so good at behaving normally that I ended up being afraid of him. How could he be so good at pretending? How could he put everyone off the scent like that? The duplicity was horrible! And what if he was the devil in a cassock?

Before the evening meal Rudy bounded over to me gleefully.

'I've got it: he's in the Resistance. He must have a radio transmitter hidden in the old chapel. Every evening he's given information and transmits it.'

'You're right!'

I liked that idea straight away because it saved Father Pons, rehabilitating the hero who had come for me when I was with the de Sullys.

At dusk Father Pons organized a game of dodgeball in the yard. I decided not to play so that I could properly admire him: free, kind, laughing, surrounded by the children he had saved from the Nazis. There was nothing evil emanating from him. Only his goodness shone through. It was blindingly obvious.

*

I slept a little better in the days that followed. I had, in fact, hated the nights ever since I arrived at the school. There, in that iron bed, between the chill sheets, beneath our dormitory's imposing ceiling, lying on a mattress so thin my bones knocked against the metal bed springs, and despite sharing the room with thirty classmates and a prefect, I felt more alone than ever.

I dreaded falling asleep, I even wouldn't allow myself to, and while this struggle went on I didn't like my own company at all. Worse than that, it disgusted me. I really was worthless, a flea, more insignificant than a cowpat. I railed at myself and scolded myself, promising myself terrible punishments: 'If you let yourself go, you'll have to give away your best marble, your red agate, to the boy you hate the most. I know, to Fernand!' But, despite my threats, I still succumbed . . . whatever precautions I took, I woke in the morning with my hips stuck to a warm wet patch with a heavy smell of cut hay, at first enjoying the feel and smell of it, even rolling in it contentedly, until the realization dawned, mercilessly, that I had wet the bed yet again! I was all the more ashamed because I had succeeded in staying dry for years by that age. Now the Villa Jaune was making me regress, and I couldn't understand why.

For a few nights – perhaps because, as I nodded off with my head on my pillow, I was thinking about Father Pons's heroism – I managed to control my bladder.

One Sunday afternoon Rudy came over with a conspiratorial look in his eye.

'I've got the key . . .'

'What key?'

'The key to the chapel, of course.'

We could now check on our hero's activities.

A few minutes later, out of breath but still keen, we were stepping inside the chapel.

It was empty.

No pews or pulpit or altar. Nothing. Roughly plastered walls. A dusty floor. Dry shrunken spider's webs. Nothing. A tired old building with nothing interesting about it at all.

We daren't look at each other, each afraid we would see our own disappointment reflected in the other's face.

'Let's go up the bell tower. If there's a radio transmitter, it'll be high up.'

We flew up the spiral staircase. But there were only a few pigeon droppings waiting for us.

'Oh come on, this can't be happening!'

Rudy stamped his foot. His hypothesis was falling apart. Father Pons was slipping through our fingers. We couldn't get to the bottom of his mystery.

What was worse for me was that I could no longer convince myself he was a hero.

'Let's go back.'

As we cut back through the woods, tormented by what Father Pons could possibly be up to every night in that empty place with no lights on, we didn't exchange a single word. I had made up my mind: I wouldn't wait another day to find out, particularly as I was risking a renewal of my bedwetting.

Night. The countryside dead. The birds silent.

At half past nine I took up my post on the stairs, with more clothes on than the last time, a scarf around my neck, and my clogs wrapped in felt stolen from the craft workshop so that I didn't make any noise.

The shadow hurried down the stairs and set off into the grounds where every outline had been erased by the darkness.

Once I reached the chapel I jumped into the clearing and tapped out the secret code on the wooden door.

The door was drawn ajar and, without waiting for a reaction, I slipped inside.

'But . . .'

Father Pons hadn't had time to identify me, he had simply seen a rather smaller than usual figure nip past. Out of habit he had closed the door behind me. So there we were, trapped in the gloom, unable to make out each other's features or even an outline.

'Who is it?' cried Father Pons.

Horrified by my own daring, I couldn't manage an answer.

'Who is it?' he said again, in a threatening voice this time.

I felt like running away. I heard a scratching sound, then a flame flared up. Father Pons's face appeared behind a match, distorted, twisted and disturbing. I backed away. The flame came closer.

'What? Is it you, Joseph?'

'Yes.'

'How dare you leave the Villa?'

'I wanted to know what you do in here.'

In one long breathless sentence I told him about my doubts, my tailing him, my questions and the empty chapel.

'Go back to your dormitory at once!'

'No.'

'You will do as you're told.'

'No. If you don't tell me what you do here, I'll start screaming and the other man will know you haven't managed to keep the secret.'

'That's blackmail, Joseph.'

Just then the knocking sounded on the door. I fell silent. Father Pons opened the door, put his head out and brought in the bag after a brief hurried discussion.

'You see, I was quiet,' I pointed out once the clandestine delivery man was far enough away. 'I'm on your side, not against you.'

'I don't tolerate spies, Joseph.'

A cloud moved away from the moon which shed its blue light into the chapel, turning our faces a grey putty colour. Father Pons suddenly seemed too tall and too thin, a great question mark traced out on a wall in charcoal, almost exactly like the Nazis' caricature of a wicked Jew seen all over our neighbourhood, his eyes so bright they were unsettling. He smiled.

'Oh, come on then!'

Taking my hand, he led me to the left-hand side of the chapel where he moved aside an old rug stiff with grime. A ring appeared in the floor. Father Pons pulled it and a flagstone opened up.

Steps led down into the dark body of the earth.

An oil lamp stood waiting on the first step. Father Pons lit it and climbed slowly into the underground space, waving me on behind him.

'What do you find beneath a church, my little Joseph?'

'A cellar?'

'A crypt.'

We had reached the last step. A cool smell of mushrooms wafted from the depths. Was this the earth breathing?

'And what do you find in a crypt?'

'I don't know.'

'A synagogue.'

He lit a few candles and the secret synagogue Father Pons had put together appeared before me. Beneath a cloak of richly embroidered cloth, he kept a scroll of the Torah, a long parchment covered in sacred writings. A photograph of Jerusalem indicated which direction to turn to when praying, because it is through that city that all prayers are taken up to God.

Behind us were shelves laden with things.

'What's all that?'

'My collection.'

He showed me prayer books, mystic poems, rabbis' commentaries, and seven- and nine-branched candlesticks. Beside a gramophone was a pile of shiny black discs.

'What are those records?'

'Prayer music, Yiddish songs. Do you know who was the first collector of human history, my little Joseph?'

'No.'

'It was Noah.'

'Never heard of him.'

'A very long time ago, the world was blighted by constant rain. The water caved in roofs and tore down walls, destroyed bridges, covered roads and swelled rivers and streams. Huge floods carried whole towns and villages away. The survivors took refuge on mountain tops, where at first they found safety but eventually the constant trickle of water caused the rock to crack and split apart. One man, Noah, predicted that our planet would be completely covered in water. So he began a collection. With the help of his sons and daughters, he managed to find a male and female of every living creature, a fox and a vixen, a tiger and a tigress, a cock pheasant and a hen pheasant, pairs of spiders, ostriches, snakes . . . everything except for fish and aquatic mammals, which were proliferating in the swelling oceans. At the same time he built a huge boat and, when the waters reached him, he loaded all the animals and all the remaining people on to the boat. For several months Noah's Ark sailed aimlessly over the vast sea that the earth's surface had become. Then the rains stopped. The water level crept down. Noah was afraid he might run out of food for those living on his ark. He released a dove which flew back with a fresh olive branch in its beak, proving that the mountain tops were at last emerging above the waves. It was then that Noah realized he had succeeded in his extraordinary challenge: to save all of God's creatures.'

'Why didn't God save them himself? Didn't he care? Had he gone away on holiday?'

'God created the universe once, once and for all. He made instinct and intelligence so that we could cope without him.'

'Are you being like Noah, then?'

'Yes. I collect things, like him. When I was a child I lived in an African country called the Belgian Congo, because my father worked there; the whites so despised the blacks that I started a collection of local black artefacts.'

'Where are they now?'

'In the museum in Namur. Thanks to a group of

painters, they've become fashionable now: it's called "Negro art". At the moment I'm working on two collections: my Romany collection and my Jewish collection. Everything Hitler wants to wipe out.'

'Wouldn't it be better to kill Hitler?'

He gave no reply but led me over to the piles of books.

'Every evening I come here to meditate over these Jewish books. And during the day, in my office, I learn Hebrew. You never know . . .'

'You never know what?'

'If the "rains" carry on, if there isn't a single Hebrew-speaking Jew left in the cosmos, I could teach it to you. And you could pass it on.'

I nodded. It was so late at night and the crypt seemed so fantastical, an Ali Baba's cave wavering in the flickering candlelight, that this all seemed more like a game to me than reality.

'Then people would say you're Noah and I'm your son!' I exclaimed in a shrill, fervent voice.

He was touched, and knelt in front of me. I could tell he wanted to put his arms around me but didn't dare. It was wonderful.

'We're going to make a deal, all right? You, Joseph, are going to pretend to be a Christian, and I'm going

67

to pretend to be a Jew. You'll go to Mass and to catechism, and you'll learn about the life of Jesus from the New Testament, while I will tell you about the Torah, the Mishnah and the Talmud, and we'll write out Hebrew letters together. All right?'

'It's a deal!'

'It's our secret, the biggest secret ever. You and I could die if we give this secret away. Do you swear you'll keep it?'

'I swear.'

I re-enacted the convoluted gestures Rudy had taught me for sealing an oath, and spat on the ground.

From that night on I was entitled to a clandestine double life with Father Pons. I hid my nocturnal expeditions from Rudy, and managed to dampen his interest in Father Pons's behaviour by turning his attention to pretty blonde sixteen-year-old Dora, an easy-going girl who worked in the kitchen and helped the bursar. I claimed she stared at Rudy whenever he wasn't looking at her. Rudy fell headfirst into the trap and became obsessed with Dora. He actively enjoyed sighing over some love-interest that was way out of his reach.

Meanwhile I was learning Hebrew with its twenty-two consonants and twelve vowels but, more particularly, I began to notice the real motives, beneath outward appearances, that were governing the school. By a clever twist in the rules, Father Pons made sure we respected the Sabbath: Saturday was a compulsory day of rest. We could only do our homework and learn our lessons after vespers on Sunday.

'For Jews, the week begins on Sunday, for Christians it's Monday.'

'How come?'

'In the Bible – which Jews presumably read just as much as Christians – it says that when God created the world he worked for six days and rested on the seventh. We should do the same. According to Jews, the seventh day is Saturday. Later, the Christians wanted to make a distinction between themselves and the Jews, who didn't accept Jesus as the Messiah, and they maintained that it was Sunday.'

'Who's right?'

'What does it matter?'

'Couldn't God tell people what he thinks?'

'What really matters isn't what God thinks of people but what people think of God.'

'Mm-yes . . . What I think is God worked for six days and then he hasn't done anything since!'

Father Pons always threw his head back and laughed at my indignant comments. I was constantly trying to minimize the differences between the two religions in order to reduce them to one; and he always deterred me from simplifying things.

'Joseph, you want to know which of the two religions is the true one. But neither of them is! A religion can't be true or false, it's a template for a way of life.'

'How do you expect me to respect religions if they're not true?'

'If you only respect the truth, then you won't have much to respect. $2 + 2 = 4$, that's the only thing you'll be able to respect. Apart from that, you'll keep coming across unreliable factors: feelings, expectations, values, choices – all fragile, fluctuating constructions. Nothing mathematical about them. Respect isn't about what's been confirmed, but what's been suggested.'

In December Father Pons's crafty double-dealing meant we celebrated the Christian festival of Christmas at the same time as the Jewish festival of Hanukkah, a trick that only the Jewish children noticed. On the one hand, we commemorated the birth of Jesus, decorated the crib in the village and attended Christian services. On the other, we had to go to a 'candle workshop' where we learned to make wicks, melt wax, dye it and mould the candles. In the evening we lit our finished works in the windows; the Christian children were, therefore, rewarded for their efforts while we Jewish children could secretly take part in the rites of Hanukkah, the Festival of Light, a time of games and gift-giving when people are expected to give alms and light candles at dusk. How many of us at the Villa Jaune were Jewish? And which of us? No one except Father Pons knew. When I had suspicions about one of my classmates, I never let myself pursue them further. Lie and let lie. That way lay safety, for all of us.

In 1943 the police descended on the Villa Jaune several times. Each time they picked a year-group and ran identity checks. Genuine or fake, our papers stood the test. Systematic searches through our cupboards failed to find anything either. No one was arrested.

All the same, Father Pons was worried.

'For now we're only dealing with the Belgian police. I know those boys, or, if not them, at least their parents; when they see it's me they daren't push things too far. But I've heard that the Gestapo are doing surprise raids . . .'

Even so, after every scare, life went back to normal. We ate little and badly, dishes made of chestnuts and potatoes, thin soups with turnips chasing each other round the bowl, and warm milk by way of pudding. We boarders got into the habit of breaking into someone's cupboard if he had received a parcel by post; then we might find a box of biscuits or a jar of jam or honey, and we had to eat it as quickly as possible for fear of being robbed of it in turn.

In the springtime, during a Hebrew lesson when we were safely locked inside his office, Father Pons was having trouble concentrating. Furrowing his brow, he even stopped hearing my questions.

'What's the matter, Father?'

'We're getting close to First Communion time, Joseph. I'm worried. I can't make the Jewish children who are old enough to take First Communion join in the ceremony with the Christians. It's impossible, I don't have the right. Not with respect to them or with respect to my faith. It would be sacrilege. What am I going to do?'

I didn't hesitate for a moment.

'Ask Mademoiselle Marcelle.'

'What makes you say that?'

'If there's one person who'll do whatever they can to get in the way of communion, it's Dammit, don't you think?'

He smiled at my suggestion.

The following day I was allowed to go with him to the pharmacy in Chemlay.

'He's such a sweetheart, that boy,' grumbled Mademoiselle Marcelle when she saw me. 'Here, catch!'

She threw me a honey-flavoured pastille.

While my teeth struggled with the sweet, Father Pons explained the situation.

'Damn it, that's no problem, Monsieur Pons. I'll give you a hand. How many of them are there?'

'Twelve.'

'You can just say they're ill! Bingo! All twelve confined to the infirmary.'

Father Pons thought it over.

'People will notice they're not there. It'll draw attention to them.'

'Not if we say there's an epidemic . . .'

'Even so. People will wonder.'

'Then you'll have to add a couple of boys above all

73

suspicion. I know, the burgomaster's son, for example. Better still, the Brognards' boy, you know, those idiots who put a picture of Hitler in the window of their cheese shop.'

'Of course! Still, you can't make fourteen boys ill just like that . . .'

'Nonsense, leave it to me.'

What did Dammit do? Claiming to be doing medical checks, she came to the infirmary and examined the group of postulants. Two days later, with their insides tormented by diarrhoea, the burgomaster's son and the Brognard boy stayed in bed, unable to get to their lessons. Dammit came and described the symptoms to Father Pons who asked the twelve Jewish communicants to imitate them.

The communion was planned for the following day and the twelve pseudo-victims were confined to the infirmary for three days.

The ceremony took place in Chemlay church, a magisterial service during which the organ thundered more than ever. I really envied my classmates in their white albs for taking part in such a show. Deep down, I promised myself I would be in their shoes one day. Father Pons could teach me the Torah all he liked, nothing touched me in the same way as Catholic

74

services with their gold and pomp, their music and that huge airborne God who hovered benevolently under the ceiling.

When we were back in the Villa Jaune – sharing the frugal banquet which seemed phantasmagorical to us because we were so hungry – I was surprised to spot Mademoiselle Marcelle in the hall. As soon as Father Pons saw her, he disappeared into his office with her.

That very evening he told me of the catastrophe we had so narrowly missed.

During the communion service the Gestapo had swooped on the boarding school. The Nazis had probably used the same reasoning as Father Pons: the fact that any child the right age to communicate was not at the ceremony was as good as a denunciation.

Luckily, Mademoiselle Marcelle was on guard outside the infirmary. When the Nazis emerged from the empty dormitories on to the top landing she started to cough and spit 'in the most revolting way', as she put it. Anyone who knew the spectacularly ugly Dammit in her natural state would shudder at the thought of such a performance. Showing no resistance to their request, she opened the door to the infirmary, warning them that the boys were very contagious. With these words she gave a poorly controlled sneeze and showered the Nazis' faces with spittle.

Anxiously wiping their faces, the Gestapo turned swiftly on their heels and left. Once the black cars had gone Mademoiselle Marcelle spent two hours bent double with laughter on a bed in the infirmary, a sight which, according to my classmates, was initially rather horrible but soon provoked an epidemic of its own.

Although he never let it show, I could tell Father Pons was more and more worried.

'I'm frightened they'll do a strip search, Joseph. What could I do if the Nazis made you strip to find the ones who are circumcised?'

I nodded and pulled a face to show that I shared his fears when, in fact, I had no idea what he was talking about. Circumcised? When I quizzed Rudy, he started sniggering with the same chuckling sounds he made if he talked about the lovely Dora, as if knocking a bag of walnuts against his chest.

'You're pulling my leg! Don't you know what circumcision is? You can't not know you've been done, surely?'

'Done?'

'Circumcised.'

The conversation was taking an unpleasant turn: once again I was attributed some special status I didn't know anything about! As if being Jewish wasn't enough!

'Your willy hasn't got skin all the way to the end, has it?'

'Of course not.'

'Well, Christians have skin hanging over the end. You can't see the rounded bit.'

'Like dogs?'

'Yup. Exactly like dogs.'

'So it's true then, that we're a completely different race!'

This information devastated me: my hopes of becoming a Christian were evaporating. Because of some scrap of skin no one could see, I was condemned to staying Jewish.

'No, you idiot,' Rudy retorted, 'there's nothing natural about it, it's a surgical procedure: it was done to you a few days after you were born. The rabbi cut your skin off.'

'Why?'

'So you could be like your father.'

'Why?'

'Because it's been like that for thousands of years.'

'Why?'

I was staggered by this discovery. That same evening I snuck off and examined my pink soft-skinned appendage for minutes on end, but learned absolutely nothing. I couldn't imagine how it could possibly be any different. Over the next few days, to check that Rudy wasn't lying to me, I parked myself by the toilets in the playground, spending all of break time washing and re-washing my hands at the basins. Out of the corner of my eye I peered into the neighbouring urinal to try and see my classmates' penises as they took them in or out of their trousers. It wasn't long before I could confirm that Rudy had been telling the truth.

'It's ridiculous, Rudy. Christians do have a bit of skin at the end, all drawn together and wrinkly, it looks like the end bit of a balloon, where you make a knot. And that's not all; they take longer than us to pee, they shake their willies afterwards. Almost as if they're annoyed with them. Are they punishing themselves?'

'No, they're shaking off the drips before putting it back in. It's harder for them to stay clean than it is for us. If they're not careful they can get loads of germs which smell and make it sore.'

'And we're the ones who are being hunted down? Does that make any sense to you?'

On the other hand, I now understood Father Pons's concern. I then noticed the invisible scheme in place for our weekly shower: Father Pons drew up lists which he checked himself as he called out the names, sending ten pupils of mixed ages at a time to get undressed and go from the changing rooms to the showers, with him alone keeping an eye on them. Each group turned out to be made up of one 'type'. A non-Jew never had an opportunity to see a Jew naked, and vice versa, as nudity was forbidden on pain of punishment anywhere else in the school. Now I could easily work out who was hiding at the Villa Jaune. From then on I was aware of the possible consequences for myself, so I got into the habit of avoiding urinals, and emptied my bladder in a locked cubicle. I even tried to redress the operation that had maimed me: I devoted time alone to manipulating the skin so that it went back to its original state and covered my glans. In vain! However roughly I pulled it, at the end of the session it would ride back up, and there was no noticeable improvement with the passing days.

'What can we do if the Gestapo get you all to undress, Joseph?'

Why did Father Pons confide in the youngest boarder? Did he think I was braver than the others? Did he need to break his silence? Was it difficult for him bearing these terrible responsibilities alone?

'I mean if the Gestapo make you all drop your trousers.'

The answer nearly did for us all in August 1943. The school, which was officially closed, turned into a holiday camp for the summer. Anyone without a host family stayed on in the boarding house until the beginning of the next school year. Instead of feeling abandoned, those of us who were left felt like princes: the Villa Jaune was ours and the long weeks of plentiful fruit went some way to easing our constant gnawing hunger. With the help of a few young seminarians, Father Pons devoted his time to us. It was a constant round of long walks, campfires, ball games and Charlie Chaplin films projected on to a white sheet held taut against the dark night in the covered yard. Although we were discreet around our supervisors, we no longer had to take any precautions amongst ourselves: we were all Jewish. Out of gratitude to Father Pons, we were all unbelievably eager about the only lessons we continued to have, our catechism lessons. We sang with tremendous enthusiasm in all Christian services and, on rainy mornings, threw ourselves into building a crib and the figures to go with it for the following Christmas.

One day when a football match had reduced all the players to a muck sweat, Father Pons ordered immediate showers.

The older boys had had theirs and the middle group too. All that remained was the youngest group, which included me.

There were about twenty of us playing and whooping under cool water streaming from the shower heads when a German officer stepped into the changing rooms.

As the blond-haired officer came in we children turned to stone, our voices dying away, and Father Pons went whiter than the tiling. Everything froze, except for the jetting water, which continued gleefully, obliviously showering us.

The officer inspected us. Some instinctively covered their genitals, a naturally modest gesture which came too late not to be seen as an admission.

The water streamed on. Silence sweated out of us in great fat droplets.

The officer had just established our identity. A

flicker of his eyes showed that he was thinking. Father Pons took a step forward.

'You were looking for . . . .?' he said in a cracked voice.

The officer explained the situation in French. Since morning his troop had been tracking a Resistance fighter who had climbed over the wall to the grounds as he fled. He was now trying to see where the intruder might be hiding.

'You can see that your fugitive isn't hiding here,' said Father Pons.

'Yes, I can see that,' the officer replied slowly.

Silence descended again, heavy with fear and danger. I grasped the fact that my life would stop there. Just a few more seconds and we would be filing out, naked, humiliated, to climb into a lorry that would take us to some destination I couldn't imagine.

There were footsteps outside. Thump of boots. Steel toecaps on paving stones. Guttural cries.

The officer in his grey-green uniform ran to the door and opened it slightly.

'He's not in here. Keep looking. *Schnell!*'

The door was already closing again, and the troop moving away.

The officer looked at Father Pons whose lips were

quivering. Some of us started to cry. My teeth were chattering.

At first I thought the officer was reaching for his revolver in his belt. In fact he was taking out his wallet.

'Here,' he said to Father Pons, handing him a banknote, 'treat the boys to some sweets.'

Father Pons was so dumbstruck he didn't respond, so the officer forcibly put the five francs into his hand, gave us a smile and a wink, clicked his heels together and strode out.

How long did the silence last after he left? How many minutes did it take for us to understand we were saved? Some carried on crying because they were still gripped with fear; others were rooted to the spot, speechless; still others rolled their eyes as if to say 'can you believe it, can any of you believe it?'

Father Pons, his face waxy and lips white, suddenly slumped to the floor. Kneeling on the soaking concrete, he rocked backwards and forwards uttering jumbled words, his eyes glazed, haunted. I threw myself at him and hugged him to me even though I was wet; it was a protective gesture, the sort of thing I would have done to Rudy.

Only then did I hear what he kept saying:

'Thank you, my Lord. Thank you, my Lord. For my children, I thank you.'

Then he turned his head towards me, seemed to become aware of me and, abandoning self-control, collapsed in my arms in tears.

Some emotions – be they happy or unhappy – prove so strong that they break us. Father Pons's relief so overwhelmed us that it had a contagious effect, and a few minutes later twelve little Jewish boys, naked as the day they were born, and one priest in his cassock were all clinging together, soaked and overwrought, laughing and crying at the same time.

A vague sense of happiness carried us through the next few days. Father Pons smiled the whole time. He confessed to me that he had drawn renewed faith from that turn of events.

'Do you really think it was God who helped us, Father?' I asked, making the most of my Hebrew lesson to voice the questions that were plaguing me. Father Pons looked at me kindly.

'To be honest, no, my little Joseph. God doesn't get involved in that sort of thing. I'm feeling happy since that German officer did what he did because I've regained some faith in human nature.'

'Well, I think it's because of you. You're in God's good books.'

'Don't talk nonsense.'

'Don't you think that if you behave in a godly way – doesn't matter if you're a good Jew or a good Christian – then nothing bad can happen to you?'

'Where did you get a silly idea like that?'

'From the catechism. Father Boniface . . .'

'Stop! That's dangerous nonsense! Humans hurt each other and God doesn't play any part in it. He made men free. So we suffer or are happy quite independently of our good qualities and our failings. What sort of terrible role are you attributing to God? Can you imagine for a single second that someone who escapes from the Nazis is loved by God, but anyone who's captured by them isn't? God doesn't meddle in our business.'

'Do you mean that, whatever happens, God couldn't care less?'

'I mean that, whatever happens, God has done what he had to do. It's up to us now. We are responsible for ourselves.'

Four

A second school year began.

Rudy and I became closer and closer. We were different in every way – age, height, concerns, attitude – but, instead of driving us apart, each of these differences only made us more aware of how much we liked each other. I helped him by clarifying his muddled ideas while he protected me from fights with his strong stature but more particularly his reputation as a bad pupil. 'You can't get anything out of him,' the teachers used to say, 'we've never come across such a hard nut to break.' Rudy was completely impermeable to any kind of learning, and we admired him for it. The teachers always managed to 'get something out of' the rest of us, which proved we were weak, corrupt and had a suspect tendency to accept compromise. They got nothing out of Rudy. The perfect dunce: pure, unadulterated, unblemished and confronting them with total resistance. He became the hero of our other war, the war of pupils against masters. And disciplinary punishments were doled out to him so frequently that his wild-eyed, unkempt head was adorned with another wreath: the crown of martyrdom.

One afternoon when he was in detention and I was passing a piece of stolen bread through the window, I asked him why, even when he was being punished, he was still passive and unwavering, and refused to learn. He opened up to me:

'There are seven of us in my family: two parents and five children. They're all intellectuals except for me. My father's a lawyer, my mother's a famous concert pianist who plays with all the best orchestras, my brothers and sisters all had diplomas by the time they were twenty. Nothing but brains . . . and all arrested. Carted off in trucks. They didn't think it could happen to them, which was why they didn't hide. Such intelligent, respectable people. What saved me was that I wasn't at home or at school! I was traipsing about the streets. Sole survivor because I'd gone walkabout . . . So, you see, studying . . .'

'Do you think I'm doing the wrong thing learning my lessons?'

'No, not you, Joseph. You've got what it takes and

you've still got life ahead of you . . .'

'Rudy, you're not yet sixteen . . .'

'I know, it's already too late.'

He didn't say any more, but I could tell he too was furious with his family. Even though they had vanished, even though they never contacted us, our parents still played a constant part in our lives at the Villa Jaune. I know I resented mine! I resented them for being Jewish, for making me Jewish, and for exposing us to danger. Crazy, the pair of them! What was my father? Hopeless. And my mother? A victim. A victim because she married my father, a victim because she failed to gauge her own terrible weakness, a victim for being just a kind, devoted wife. I may have felt contempt for my mother, but I still forgave her because I couldn't help loving her. On the other hand, I was pervaded by a hefty hatred towards my father. He had forced me to be his son without showing any ability to ensure I had a decent fate. Why wasn't I Father Pons's son?

One afternoon in November 1943, Rudy and I climbed up into the branches of an old oak tree that overlooked the surrounding countryside with its great spread of fields laid out before our eyes. We were scrutinizing the bark to find the nests where squirrels hibernated. Our feet skimmed the top of the wall around the grounds; if we had wanted to we could have escaped, jumping down on to the path round the perimeter and running away. But where to? Nothing was worth more than our safety at the Villa Jaune. We kept our adventures within its walls. While Rudy heaved himself higher up, I parked myself on the first fork in the branches and, from there, I thought I caught sight of my father.

A tractor was coming down the road, heading straight past us. There was a man at the wheel: even though he had no beard and was dressed like a farm-worker, he looked enough like my father for me to recognize him. And I did recognize him.

I was transfixed. I didn't want this to be happening. 'Please don't let him see me!' I held my breath. The tractor spluttered under our tree and trundled on towards the valley. 'Phew, he didn't see me!' But he was only ten metres away and I could still have called out to him, caught him in time.

With a dry mouth and holding my breath, I waited till the machine had become tiny and inaudible in the distance. When I was quite sure it had gone, I came back to life: I breathed out, blinked, shuddered. Rudy sensed that I was upset.

'What's the matter?'

'I thought I saw someone I knew on the tractor.'

'Who?'

'My father.'

'You poor thing, that's impossible!'

I shook my head to get the stupid idea out of my brain.

'Of course it's impossible . . .'

Wanting Rudy to feel sorry for me, I put on a face like a disappointed child. In fact, I was delighted I had avoided my father. Besides, was it actually him? Rudy must have been right. Could we live only a few kilometres apart without realizing it? Not likely! By nightfall I was convinced I'd dreamed it. And I erased the episode from my memory.

Several years later, I found out that it was in fact my father who had come so close to me that day. My father whom I rejected, my father whom I wished was far away, not there, dead even . . . I can try justifying that wilful contempt – a monstrous response to him – with my vulnerability and panic at the time, but I will still feel the full, searing, burning shame of it till my dying day.

*

When we met in his secret synagogue Father Pons would give me news of the war.

'Now that the Germans are getting caught up in Russia and the Americans have joined the fight, I think Hitler's going to lose. But at what cost? The Nazis here are more and more frantic, tracking down the Resistance with furious determination, driven by despair. I'm very frightened for all of us, Joseph, really very frightened.'

He could sense some threat hanging in the air, the way a dog can sense a wolf.

'It's all right, Father, everything's going to be OK. Let's keep on with our work.'

I had the same tendency to be protective with Father Pons as with Rudy. I loved them both so much that, to quell their anxieties, I adopted a reassuring and unshakeable optimism.

'Can you make the difference between Jews and Christians clearer for me, Father?'

'Jews and Christians believe in the same God, the God who dictated the Ten Commandments to Moses. But Jews don't recognize Jesus as the promised Messiah, a longed-for envoy from God; they see him as just another Jewish sage. You become a Christian the moment you feel that Jesus really is the Son of

God, that God was incarnate in him, and died and rose again in him.'

'So for the Christians that's already happened; for the Jews it's still to come.'

'That's it, Joseph. Christians remember while Jews live in hope.'

'So a Christian is a Jew who's stopped waiting?'

'Yes. And a Jew is a Christian from before Jesus.'

I was quite tickled by the idea that I was a 'Christian from before Jesus'. What with the Catholic catechism and my clandestine initiation in the Torah, religious history captured my imagination more than the childish tales borrowed from the library: it seemed more physical, more intimate, more concrete. After all, these were my ancestors, Moses, Abraham, David, John the Baptist, even Jesus! The blood of one of these men probably flowed through my veins. And their lives were never bland, no more than mine was: they fought and shouted, wept and sung, they risked their own lives at every turn. What I didn't dare admit to Father Pons was that I had incorporated him in this history. I couldn't picture Pontius Pilate, the Roman procurator who washed his hands, with any other face but his: it seemed quite logical to me that Father Pons should be there in the Gospels, so close to Jesus, somewhere between the Jews and the future Christians, a confused intermediary, an honest man not sure how to choose.

I could tell that Father Pons was disconcerted by the studies he subjected himself to for my sake. Like many Catholics, he previously knew extremely little about the Old Testament and discovered it with a sense of wonderment, as he did passages from rabbis' commentaries.

'Joseph, some days I wonder whether I wouldn't do better to be a Jew,' he would say, his eyes bright with emotion.

'No, Father, stay a Christian, you don't know how lucky you are.'

'Jewish religion puts its emphasis on respect, Christian religion on love. And I'm beginning to wonder: isn't respect more fundamental than love? And more achievable too . . . Loving your enemy, as Jesus suggests, and turning the other cheek, I admire all that but it's hard to do. Particularly at the moment. Would you turn the other cheek to Hitler, Joseph?'

'Never!'

'Neither would I! It's true I'm not worthy of Christ. It would take more than my whole lifetime to be like him . . . And yet, can love be a duty? Can we rule our own hearts? I don't think so. According to the great rabbis, respect is higher than love. It is a constant obligation. That strikes me as possible. I can respect people I don't like and those I don't mind about. But love them? Anyway, do I really need to love them if I respect them? Love's difficult, you can't produce it at will or control it or deliberately make it last. Whereas respect . . .'

He scratched his smooth scalp.

'I wonder whether we Christians are just rather sentimental Jews . . .'

And so my life went on, punctuated by my studies, our sublime reflections on the Bible, my fear of the Nazis, the antics of the Resistance which was becoming stronger and more daring every day, games with my classmates and walks with Rudy. Chemlay was not spared in the bombing, but the English pilots avoided the Villa Jaune, possibly because it was a long way from the station, but almost certainly because Father Pons had taken the precaution of raising a Red Cross flag on the lightning conductor. Paradoxically, I really enjoyed air raids: I never went down into the shelters with my friends but, along with Rudy, I watched the show from the roof. The

Royal Air Force jets flew so low we could see the pilots and wave to them.

In times of war the greatest danger is growing used to it. Particularly becoming accustomed to danger itself.

Dozens of people in Chemlay challenged the Nazi occupation with clandestine activities, eventually underestimating their strength; as a result of this the announcement of the Normandy landings cost us dearly.

When we heard that waves of well-armed American troops had set foot on the continent we were intoxicated by the news. Even though we had to keep the fact quiet, we couldn't wipe the telltale smiles off our faces. Father Pons seemed to be walking on air, like Jesus on water, happiness radiating from his features.

That Sunday we couldn't wait to go to Mass, longing to share this near victory with the locals, at least by exchanging meaningful looks. We all lined up in the playground a quarter of an hour early.

Along the way, farm workers in their Sunday best winked at us; one woman gave me some chocolate; another put an orange into my hand; a third slipped a piece of cake in my pocket.

'Why's it always Joseph?' grumbled a classmate.

''Course it is, he's the handsomest!' Rudy called from the far end.

It was just as well: my tummy was constantly empty, especially as I was having a growth spurt.

I waited for the moment when we would pass the pharmacy because I suspected that Mademoiselle Marcelle – who, along with Father Pons, had saved and protected so many children – would be beaming. Perhaps she would be so happy she would toss me a few boiled sweets?

But the metal shutter was down over her windows.

Our group reached the village square early and then everyone, schoolboys and locals alike, stopped dead in front of the church.

Through the wide-open doors we heard rousing music surging from the organ pipes, which were blasting at full volume. I recognized the refrain in disbelief: our Belgian national anthem!

The crowd stood rooted to the spot. Playing our national anthem like that right under the Nazis' noses was the ultimate outrage. It was as good as saying: 'Get out, run away, you've lost, you're nothing now!'

Who would dare be that insolent?

The first to see her started to mutter amongst

themselves: Dammit! With her hands on the keyboards and her feet on the pedals, Mademoiselle Marcelle had set foot in a church for the first time in years so she could tell the Nazis they were going to lose the war.

Euphoric and excited, we stood around the church as if watching some dazzling and dangerous circus act. Dammit played damn well! Much better than the anaemic organist who did the services. In her hands the instrument boomed like a barbaric fanfare, all red and gold with a blaring brass section and virile drums. The notes rolled out to us powerfully, reverberating through the ground and making shop windows rattle.

All at once there was a screech of tyres. A black car braked in front of the church and four characters leaped out.

The Gestapo officers grabbed Mademoiselle Marcelle who stopped playing but started hurling insults at them:

'You've had it! It's over! You can lay into me but it won't change anything. You're pathetic! Nancy boys! Impotent!'

The Nazis bundled her unceremoniously into the car, and it set off.

Father Pons, paler than ever, made a sign of the

cross. My fists were clenched, I wanted to run after the car, catch it up, punch the bastards. I grabbed his hand, it was icy cold.

'She'll never say anything, Father. I'm sure she won't say anything.'

'I know, Joseph, I know. Dammit is the bravest of us all. But what will they do to her?'

We didn't have to wait long for the answer. At eleven o'clock that same evening, the Villa Jaune was raided by the Gestapo.

Mademoiselle Marcelle, even under torture, had not said a word. All the same, during a search of her house, the Nazis had rooted out the negatives of the photographs used on our false papers.

We had been unmasked. No need even to drop our trousers. All the Nazis had to do was open our passports and they could identify the impostors.

Within twenty minutes all the Jewish children at the Villa Jaune had been gathered into one dormitory.

The Nazis were exultant. We were gripped with terror. I was so terrified I couldn't think straight. Without even realizing it, I meekly obeyed their instructions.

'Against the wall, with your hands up. Quickly!'

Rudy slipped in beside me but it did nothing to reassure me: his eyes were popping out of his head in fear.

Father Pons threw himself into the fray.

'Officers, this is an outrage: I didn't know who they were! I never guessed for a moment these boys might be Jews. They were sent to me as Aryans, true Aryans. I've been tricked, made a fool of, my credibility has been damaged.'

Even though I didn't immediately understand Father Pons's attitude, I was sure he wasn't trying to plead his own innocence to avoid arrest.

'Who brought these children here?' the officer in charge asked curtly.

Father Pons hesitated. Ten long seconds crawled by.

'I'm not going to lie to you: all these children were brought to me by Mademoiselle Marcelle, the pharmacist.'

'Didn't you find that surprising?'

'She's always entrusted orphans to my care. She's been doing it for fifteen years. Since long before the war. She's a good person. She had connections with a charity that works with disadvantaged children.'

'And who paid their fees?'

Father Pons's face drained of all colour.

'An envelope arrives every month for each child, in his name. You can check the accounts.'

'Where did these envelopes come from?'

'From our patrons . . . Who else would it be? It's all in our files. You'll find the references.'

The Nazis believed him. Their leader was drooling just at the thought of getting his hands on those lists. But Father Pons didn't falter, he turned on the attack.

'Where are you taking them?'

'To Malines.'

'And then?'

'None of your business.'

'Will it be a long journey?'

'Bound to be.'

'Well, let me sort out their things, pack their cases, get them properly dressed and give them something to eat for the journey. My sons, we can't treat children like this. If you'd put your children in my care, would you be happy for me to let them leave just like that?'

The officer with the sweaty hands hesitated and Father Pons made the most of this pause:

'I know you don't mean them any harm. Come on, I'll get everything organized and you can come and pick them up at dawn.'

Trapped by the emotional blackmail and disarmed by the priest's naïvety, the Gestapo officer wanted to prove that he himself wasn't a bad man.

'At seven o'clock on the dot tomorrow morning, they'll be washed, dressed, fed and lined up in the playground with their luggage,' Father Pons insisted gently. 'Don't make this difficult for me. I've been looking after them for years: when a child is put in my care he is in safe hands, I can be trusted.'

The Gestapo leader glanced quickly over the thirty or so Jewish children in their nightshirts, realized he wouldn't have lorries before morning, thought how tired he was feeling, shrugged and said grudgingly:

'All right, Father, I trust you.'

'You can, my son. Go in peace.'

The Gestapo men in their black uniforms left the school.

Once Father Pons was sure they were far enough away he turned to us.

'Boys,' he said, 'no screaming or panicking: you're going to get your clothes in silence, and get dressed. Then you're running away.'

There was a long sigh of collective relief. We gathered our things in silence. When we were done,

Father Pons called his helpers, five young seminarians, from the other dormitories, and shut them in the room with us.

'My sons,' he said, 'I need your help.'

'You can depend on us, Father.'

'I want you to lie.'

'But . . .'

'You have to lie. In the name of Christ. Tomorrow I want you to tell the Gestapo that masked Resistance fighters raided the villa shortly after they left. You'll say that you put up a fight. And, actually, to prove your innocence, you'll be found tied to the beds here. Do you agree to being tied up?'

'You can even punch us about a bit, Father.'

'Thank you, my sons. I'm not against punches on condition that you do it yourselves.'

'And what will happen to you?'

'I can't stay here with you. The Gestapo will no longer believe me by tomorrow. They'll want someone to blame. So I'm going to escape with the children. Of course, you'll tell them that I tipped off the Resistance and was in cahoots with them.'

The next few minutes saw the most extraordinary show I have ever witnessed. The young seminarians set about punching each other with amazing diligence, concentration and precision, one on the nose, another on the lips or an eye, and all asking for more if they felt they weren't looking battered enough. Then Father Pons tied them firmly to the bed ends and stuffed rags in their mouths.

'Can you breathe?'

They nodded. Some had bruises on their faces, others blood coming from their noses, all had tears in their eyes.

'Thank you, my sons,' said Father Pons. 'And to help you hold out till morning, think of Our Lord Jesus Christ.'

With that, he checked that each of us had a small piece of luggage and then led us down the stairs and out of the back door in total silence.

'Where are we going?' whispered Rudy.

Although I was probably the only one who had any idea, I kept it to myself.

We cut across the grounds to the clearing and Father Pons stopped us there.

'My children, I'm sorry if you think I'm mad: we're not going any further than this.'

He explained his plan and we spent the rest of the night putting it into action.

Half of us went to get some sleep in the crypt

under the chapel. The other half, which included me, spent the next few hours erasing the true clues and establishing false ones. The ground was soaked from recent rain and sank under our feet with a squelching sound: it couldn't have been easier to leave a beautiful trail.

So our group walked on through the clearing and left the park through the narrow doorway. Then, digging our heels into the soft soil, snapping the odd branch and even deliberately dropping a few belongings, we went down across the fields to the river. There Father Pons took us over to a jetty.

'Right, they'll think there was a boat waiting for us here . . . Now we're going to head back but we'll have to walk backwards, boys, so they think there were twice as many of us and so we don't leave any footprints going in the wrong direction.'

The walk back was slow and laborious: we slipped and fell – hard work on top of our fear and mounting tiredness. Back at the clearing, we still had the most difficult bit to do: hiding any trace of our footprints towards the disused chapel by beating the damp ground with foliage.

Dawn was just breaking when we joined our sleeping classmates in the crypt. Father Pons carefully closed the door and the trapdoor overhead, lighting just a single candle as a night light.

'Go to sleep, my children. There's no bell to get you up this morning.'

Not far from where I had flopped to the ground, he cleared a space for himself between some piles of books which he stacked around him like a brick wall. When he saw me watching I asked,

'Can I come into your room with you, Father?'

'Come, my little Joseph.'

I slipped in beside him and lay my cheek on his lean shoulder. I barely had time to feel his kindly smile on me before falling asleep.

The following morning the Gestapo swarmed into the Villa Jaune, came across the bound and gagged seminarians, screamed in frustration, followed our false trail down to the river and carried on looking for us beyond that point. It never occurred to them that we might not have fled.

It was now impossible for Father Pons to show himself above ground. It would also be impossible for us to stay in the secret synagogue set up beneath the chapel. We were very glad to be alive but now it was living itself that posed all sorts of problems: talking, eating, relieving ourselves. Even sleep offered no refuge because we could only lie on the bare ground and had to take it in turns.

'You see, Joseph,' Father Pons said good-humouredly, 'the time they spent on Noah's Ark can't have been a barrel of laughs.'

It was not long before the Resistance came for us one by one, to hide us elsewhere. Rudy was among the first to leave – possibly because he took up so much space! Father Pons never pointed me out to the people who came to take us. Was this deliberate? I liked to think he was keeping me with him as long as possible.

'Maybe the Allies will win sooner than we think? Maybe we'll soon be saved?' he would say with a wink.

He used these days and weeks to improve his and my knowledge of the Jewish faith.

'Your lives aren't just your lives, they bear a message. I can't let you be exterminated. We must work.'

One day when there were only five of us left in the crypt, I pointed to my three sleeping classmates and said:

'Father, I wouldn't want to die with them.'

'Why not?'

'Because, even though I live with them, they're not my friends. What have I got in common with them? Just the fact that we're victims.'

'Why are you telling me this, Joseph?'

'Because I'd rather die with you.'

I let my head loll against his knee and confided in him.

'I'd rather die with you because I like you best. I'd rather die with you because I don't want to cry over you or, worse, for you to cry over me. I'd rather die with you because then you'd be the last person I saw in the world. I'd rather die with you because, without you, I'm not going to like heaven, I'd even find it scary.'

Just then someone drummed on the door of the chapel.

'Brussels has been liberated! We've won! The English have liberated Brussels!'

Father Pons leaped to his feet and took me in his arms.

'Liberated! Did you hear that, Joseph? We're free! The Germans are withdrawing!'

The other children woke up.

The Resistance let us out of the crypt and we

started running and jumping through the streets of Chemlay, laughing all the way. Whoops of joy came from every house, people fired gunshots into the sky, unfurled flags from their windows, started dancing in the streets and bringing out bottles of alcohol that had been hidden for five years.

I stayed in Father Pons's arms right through till the evening. As he discussed the events with all the locals he wept tears of joy. I wiped them for him. This was a day for celebrations so I was allowed to be nine years old, and to sit like a child on the shoulders of the man who had saved me; I was allowed to kiss his salty pink cheeks, allowed to laugh out loud for no particular reason. I stayed with him all day, glowing with happiness. Even if I was heavy, he never complained.

'The war will be over soon.'

'The Americans are advancing towards Liège.'

'Long live the Americans!'

'Long live the English!'

'Long live all of us!'

'Hurray!'

Ever since that day, 4 September 1944, I've always believed that Brussels was liberated because I had suddenly declared my love for Father Pons. It had a profound effect on me. Since then I have always expected firecrackers to go off and flags to come out when I have declared my feelings for a woman.

Five

The next few days proved more dangerous and murderous in our region than the war itself. During the Occupation the enemy had been clearly visible and, therefore, in our sights; during the Liberation shots were fired from all quarters – neither controlled nor controllable – and chaos reigned. Having brought the children back home to the Villa Jaune, Father Pons barred us from leaving the grounds. But Rudy and I couldn't resist hauling ourselves up into our oak tree whose branches reached over the wall. Gaps in the foliage gave us a view over the plain, a bare expanse stretching to farms in the distance. From there, although we couldn't watch actual fighting, we could see its effects. That was how I came to see the German officer who had chosen not to denounce us in the showers; he was taken past in an open-topped car, in his shirt-sleeves, splattered with blood, his face bruised and head shaved, held by armed liberators taking him to face some retribution I couldn't bear to imagine.

Provisions were still a constant problem. To quell our hunger, Rudy and I took to looking through the lawn for a dark green grass with thicker leaves than the rest; we would pick a handful before popping the whole bunch into our mouths. It was bitter, disgusting, but at least we felt we had a mouthful.

Gradually things went back to normal. But no good news came with that. Mademoiselle Marcelle, the pharmacist, had been subjected to appalling torture before being deported to the East. How would she get back? Would she get back at all? For we now heard confirmation of what we had suspected during the war: the Nazis had been assassinating their prisoners in their concentration camps. Millions of human beings had been slaughtered, shot, gassed, burned or buried alive.

I started wetting the bed again. Terror was now retrospective: I was horrified by the fate I had been spared. Shame became retrospective too: I thought about my father, how I had glimpsed him but hadn't see fit to call out to him. Had it really been him? Was he still alive? And my mother? I started loving them all over again with a love multiplied ten times by my remorse.

On cloudless nights I would leave the dormitory to go and gaze at the sky. When I stared at 'Joseph and Maman's star', all the stars seemed to start singing in Yiddish again. My eyes would soon blur with tears, I couldn't breathe, lying pinned to the grass with my arms outstretched, eventually choking on snot and tears.

Father Pons no longer had time for my Hebrew lessons. He spent months chasing about from morning till night, tracking down our parents, tackling the encrypted registers set up by Resistance networks, and applying to Brussels for lists of deported people who had died.

For some, news came quickly: they were the only survivors in their families. Outside lessons we comforted them and took care of them while, deep down, we worried for ourselves: Will I be next? When it takes this long, is it good news? Or the worst?

Once facts started being substituted for hopes, Rudy made up his mind he had lost all his loved ones. 'I'm so *schlemazel*, that's the only possible outcome.' Sure enough, Father Pons came back week after week with grim confirmation that his elder brother, then his other brothers, then his sister and finally his father had been gassed in Auschwitz. Each time my friend was crushed by towering silent pain: we spent hours at a time lying on the grass, holding hands and looking up at the sky full of sunlight and swallows. I think he cried but I didn't dare look for fear of humiliating him.

One evening Father Pons came back from Brussels bright red in the face from pedalling so quickly, and ran over to Rudy.

'Rudy, your mother's alive! She'll be getting to Brussels on Friday, in a convoy of survivors.'

That night Rudy was so racked with sobs of relief that I thought he would die, suffocated by his own tears, before he even managed to see his mother again.

On the Friday Rudy was out of bed before dawn to get washed and dressed, polish his shoes and do himself up like a smart townie with neatly waved, slicked-back hair, so that he was only recognizable by his prominent ears. He was so excited he couldn't stop chattering, skipping from one subject to another, leaving sentences half finished so he could get on to the next.

As he had arranged to borrow a car, Father Pons

decided I should join in the journey so, for the first time in three years, I put aside anxieties about my own family's fate.

In Brussels light rain, a dusting of water, wafted between the grey buildings, misting the car windows with a transparent veil, and making the pavements shine. When we arrived at the big, smart hotel where survivors were being dropped off, Rudy hurried over to the red- and gold-liveried concierge.

'Where's the piano? I need to take my mother to it. She's a fantastic pianist. A virtuoso. She gives concerts.'

Once we had located the long, lacquered instrument in the bar, we were told the survivors had already arrived and, having been deloused and disinfected, were being given a meal in the restaurant.

Rudy ran all the way there, accompanied by Father Pons and myself.

There, stooped over bowls of soup, scrawny men and women with dull skin clinging unbearably to their bones, all with the same rings under the same vacant eyes, and so exhausted they could barely hold their spoons. They paid no attention to us at all because they were so frantic to feed themselves, afraid someone might try and stop them.

Rudy scoured the room. 'She's not here. Is there another restaurant, Father?'

A voice rang out from one of the benches.

'Rudy!'

A woman stood up and almost collapsed as she waved to us.

'Rudy!'

'Maman!'

Rudy ran over to the woman calling to him, and took her in his arms.

I couldn't reconcile her with the mother Rudy had described to me; a tall regal woman, he had said, with a magnificent bosom, steel blue eyes, and long thick luxuriant black hair that people couldn't help admiring. Instead he was hugging a little old lady who was almost bald, with staring, frightened, washed-out grey eyes, and whose wide, flat, bony body showed through her woollen dress.

But there they were whispering Yiddish sweet nothings in each other's ears, and crying on each other's shoulders, and I concluded that Rudy might not have got the wrong person but had probably embellished his memories.

He wanted to take her away.

'Come on, Maman, there's a piano in this hotel.'

'No, Rudy, I want to finish my meal first.'

'Come on, Maman, come here.'

'I haven't finished the carrots,' she said, stamping her foot like a stubborn child.

Rudy was taken aback: this wasn't his domineering mother any more but a little girl who didn't want to miss out on her food. Gently touching Rudy's arm, Father Pons suggested he should respect her wishes.

She finished her soup slowly, conscientiously, dipping some bread into the broth, wiping the china bowl till it was spotless, oblivious to everyone else. All the survivors around her polished their plates with the same application. Underfed for years, they now ate with brutal passion.

Then Rudy helped her stand up by offering her his arm, and he introduced us. Even though she was exhausted, she had the good grace to smile at us.

'You know,' she told Father Pons, 'I only kept myself alive because I clung to the hope of seeing Rudy again.'

Rudy blinked and changed the subject.

'Come on, Maman, let's go over to the piano.'

He led her through the hotel's grand sitting rooms, with their alabaster columns and doorways swathed with heavy silk curtains, sat her carefully on the piano stool, and lifted the lid of the piano.

She gazed at that concert grand with some emotion, then wariness. Could she still play? She dragged her foot towards the pedal and stroked the keys with her fingers. She was shaking. She was frightened.

'Play, Maman, play!' murmured Rudy.

She looked at Rudy in panic. She daren't tell him she was afraid she couldn't do it, wouldn't have the strength, didn't know how to . . .

'Play, Maman, play. That's how *I* got through the war, thinking that one day you'd play for me again.'

She swayed, steadied herself on the frame, then contemplated the keyboard like some obstacle she had to overcome. Her hands moved over, shyly, then came down gently on the ivory keys.

And then came the sweetest, saddest lament I have ever heard. A bit shaky, a bit haphazard at first, then richer, more assured as the music blossomed, intensified, developed, devastating, passionate.

As she played, Rudy's mother came back to life. Beneath the woman I saw with my eyes, I could make out the one Rudy had described to me.

At the end of the piece she turned to her son.

'Chopin,' she whispered. 'He never experienced what we've been through but somehow he felt it all.'

Rudy kissed her neck.

'Will you take up your studies again, Rudy?'

'I promise I will.'

Over the next few weeks I saw Rudy's mother regularly because an old woman in Chemlay had agreed to take her in as a paying guest. She gradually got her colour and shape back, as well as her hair and air of authority. Rudy went to spend the evenings with her and stopped being the determined dunce he had always been, even displaying a remarkable aptitude for maths.

On Sundays the Villa Jaune became a gathering place for all the children who had been hidden. Children aged from three to sixteen who had not yet been claimed by their families were brought in from the surrounding area. They paraded on a makeshift stage set up in the covered yard. Lots of people would come, some to find a son or daughter, others a niece or nephew, still others searching for more distant relations for whom, after the Holocaust, they now felt responsible. Couples wanting to adopt orphans also put their names down.

I longed for these mornings as much as I dreaded them. Every time I walked across the stage after my name had been announced I hoped to hear a cry, my mother's cry. Every time I headed back in that polite silence, I wanted to mutilate myself.

'Oh Father, it's my fault my parents haven't come back: I didn't think about them during the war.'

'Don't talk nonsense, Joseph. If your parents don't come back, then it's Hitler's and the Nazis' fault. But not yours or theirs.'

'Don't you want to put me up for adoption?'

'It's too soon, Joseph. Without papers certifying that your parents are dead, I wouldn't be allowed to.'

'No one would want me, anyway!'

'Come on, you must keep on hoping.'

'I hate hoping. I feel useless and pathetic when I hope.'

'Be more humble and hope just a little bit.'

That Sunday, after the ritual orphan fair, un-rewarded and humiliated yet again, I decided to go along with Rudy to see his mother for tea in the village.

We were walking down the path when I saw two

figures in the distance climbing the hill.

Without making the decision, I started running. My feet weren't touching the ground. I could have been flying. I was going so quickly I was afraid my legs might come away at the hip.

I hadn't recognized the man or the woman: I had recognized my mother's coat. A green and pink tartan coat with a hood. Maman! My maman! I'd never seen anyone else wear that green and pink tartan coat with a hood.

'Joseph!'

I threw myself at my parents. Breathless, unable to utter a single word, I touched them and felt them and hugged them to me, I checked them, I held on to them and stopped them leaving. I kept on and on making the same uncoordinated gestures. Yes, I could feel them and touch them, yes, they really were alive.

I was so happy it hurt.

'Joseph, my Joseph! Mischke, look how handsome he is!'

'You've grown, my son.'

They said silly, meaningless things that made me cry. And I couldn't say a thing. Three years' worth of pain – that was how long we had been apart – had come piling on to my shoulders and floored me. With my mouth open forming a long silent cry, all I could manage was sobbing.

When they realized I wasn't answering any of their questions, my mother turned to Rudy.

'My Josephshi is just overcome, isn't he?'

Rudy nodded. Having my mother understand me, read me like that, brought on another wave of tears.

It was more than an hour before I recovered the power of speech. For that whole hour I wouldn't let them go, one hand clutching my father's arm, the other buried in my mother's palm. During that hour I learned, from what they told Father Pons, how they had survived, not far from there, hidden on a huge farm where they worked as farm labourers. They took so long to find me because, once back in Brussels, they discovered that the Comte and Comtesse de Sully had disappeared, and the Resistance sent them on a false trail for me that took them all the way to Holland.

As they told the story of their eventful travels, my mother kept looking round at me, stroking my face and whispering, 'My little Josephshi . . .'

I was so overcome hearing Yiddish again, a language so gentle you can't even call a child by his name without adding a caress, a diminutive, a syllable that lilts in your ear, like a sweet wrapped up in the middle of the word . . . On a diet like that, I started feeling better and all I could think of was showing them round my world, the Villa Jaune and its grounds, where I had spent such happy years.

When they had finished their story, they turned to me.

'We're going back to Brussels. Can you get your things?'

And that was when I regained the power of speech.

'What? Can't I stay here?'

My question was greeted with silent consternation. My mother blinked, not sure she had heard properly, my father stared at the ceiling, clenching his jaw, and Father Pons stretched his neck towards me.

'What did you say, Joseph?'

I suddenly understood how terrible what I had said sounded to my parents' ears. I was flooded with shame! Too late! Even so, I said it again, hoping that the second time would have a different effect to the first.

'Can't I stay here?'

Uh-oh! It was worse! Their eyes filled with tears; they looked away towards the window; Father Pons's eyebrows shot up in surprise.

'Do you realize what you're saying, Joseph?'

'I'm saying I want to stay here.'

The slap struck me before I could see it coming. Father Pons, his hand smarting, looked at me sadly. I looked at him, astonished: he had never hit me before.

'I'm sorry, Father,' I mumbled.

He shook his head sternly to mean that wasn't the reaction he wanted; he flicked his eyes at my parents. I did as I was told.

'I'm sorry, Papa. I'm sorry, Maman. It was just my way of saying I was happy here, my way of saying thank you.'

My parents opened their arms to me.

'You're right, my darling,' said my mother. 'We'll never be able to thank Father Pons enough.'

'That's right,' agreed my father.

'Have you heard, Mischke, he's lost his accent, our Josephshi has. You wouldn't know he was our son.'

'He's right, though. We should stop all this wretched Yiddish business.'

I interrupted the conversation by staring straight at Father Pons and explaining, 'I just meant it's going to be hard leaving you . . .'

*

Back in Brussels, it was all very well happily exploring the spacious house my father had rented now that he had started up in business with vengeful energy, and it was all very well succumbing to my mother's caresses, her gentleness and her lilting intonations, but I felt lonely, drifting in a boat without any oars. Brussels was huge, endless, open to the four winds, lacking the boundary wall that I would have found reassuring. I could eat my fill, and wore clothes and shoes that fitted properly, I was amassing quite a collection of toys and books in the beautiful bedroom that was for me alone, but I missed the hours spent with Father Pons thinking about the world's great mysteries. My new school friends seemed insipid, my teachers robotic, my lessons meaningless, my home boring. You can't settle back down with your parents just by kissing them. Over three years they had become strangers to me, probably because they had changed, probably because I had changed. They had lost a child and got back an adolescent. The hunger for material success that now drove my father had altered him so much that I had trouble recognizing the humble, plaintive tailor from Schaerbeek beneath the prosperous new import-export entrepreneur.

'You'll see, my son, I'm going to make a fortune,

and you can just take over the business later,' he announced, his eyes shining with excitement.

Did I want to be like him?

When he suggested preparing for my bar mitzvah by signing me up for a cheder, a traditional Jewish school, I instantly refused.

'Don't you want your bar mitzvah?'

'No.'

'Don't you want to learn to read the Torah, and to write and pray in Hebrew?'

'No.'

'Why not?'

'I want to become a Catholic!'

The response wasn't long in coming: a swift, sharp, violent slap. The second in only a few weeks. After Father Pons, my own father. For me, liberation meant mostly liberating people's slapping hand.

He called my mother and asked her to listen. I said it again, I confirmed that I wanted to adopt the Catholic faith. She cried and screamed. That same evening I ran away.

By bike, and going the wrong way several times, I retraced the journey to Chemlay, and reached the Villa Jaune at about eleven o'clock.

I didn't even ring at the gate. Skirting round the

outside wall, I pushed open the rusty door in the clearing and went to the disused chapel.

The door was open. So was the trapdoor.

As I thought he would be, Father Pons was down in the crypt.

He opened his arms wide when he saw me. I threw myself at him and unburdened all my emotion.

'You deserve another slap from me,' he said, hugging me gently.

'What's got into you all?'

He waved me to a chair and lit some candles.

'Joseph, you're one of the last survivors of a glorious people that has just been massacred. Six million Jews were assassinated . . . six million! You can't hide away from all those bodies.'

'What have I got in common with them, Father?'

'You were brought to life alongside them, and threatened with death at the same time as them.'

'And then what? I'm allowed to think differently to them, aren't I?'

'Of course you are. But, now that they no longer exist, you have to testify to the fact that they *did* exist.'

'Why me and not you?'

'I do too, just as much as you do. Each in our own way.'

'I don't want a bar mitzvah. I want to believe in Jesus Christ, like you.'

'Listen, Joseph, you'll have a bar mitzvah because you love your mother and respect your father. As for religion, you can see about that later.'

'But . . .'

'It's really important that you accept that you're Jewish now. It's nothing to do with religious faith. Later, if you still want to, you can be a converted Jew.'

'So still a Jew, a Jew for ever?'

'Yes. A Jew for ever. Have your bar mitzvah, Joseph. Otherwise you'll break your parents' hearts.'

I could tell he was right.

'You know, Father, I liked being a Jew with you.'

He burst out laughing.

'Me too, Joseph, I liked being a Jew with you.'

We laughed together for a while. Then he took me by the shoulders.

'Your father loves you, Joseph. He may not love you very well or it may be in a way you don't like, but he still loves you as he'll never love anyone else and as no one else will ever love you.'

'Not even you?'

'Joseph, I love you as much as any other child, perhaps a bit more. But it's not the same love.'

From the sense of relief washing over me, I knew that these were the words I had come to hear.

'Set yourself free from me, Joseph. I've finished my job. We can be friends now.'

He waved his arm around the crypt.

'Haven't you noticed anything?'

Despite the poor light, I could see that the candlesticks had gone, so had the Torah, the picture of Jerusalem . . . I went over to the piles of books on the shelves.

'What! . . . They're not Hebrew any more . . .'

'It's not a synagogue any more.'

'What's going on?'

'I'm starting a collection.'

He fingered a few books with unfamiliar characters on them.

'Stalin will eventually kill the soul of Russia: I'm collecting works by dissident poets.'

Father Pons was giving up on us! He must have seen the reproachful look in my eye.

'I'm not abandoning you, Joseph. *You* are there now for the Jews. You're Noah from now on.'

Six

I'm finishing writing this on a shady terrace, looking out over a sea of olive trees. Instead of withdrawing inside for a siesta with my friends, I have stayed out in the heat, because the sun injects some of its happiness into my heart.

Fifty years have passed since these events. In the end I did have a bar mitzvah, I did take over my father's business and I didn't convert to Christianity. I took up the religion of my forefathers with passion, and passed it on to my children. But God never showed up . . .

Never in all my years as a pious Jew and then an indifferent Jew have I found the God that I felt as a child in that little country church, somewhere between the magical stained-glass windows, the garland-bearing angels and the booming organ. The kindly God hovering above bouquets of lilies, gentle flames and the smell of waxed wood, and watching over hidden children and complicit villagers.

I never stopped seeing Father Pons. I first went back to Chemlay in 1948 when the local council named a street after Mademoiselle Marcelle who never returned from deportation. We were all there, all the children she had gathered up, fed and given false papers. Before unveiling the plaque dedicated to her, the burgomaster gave a speech about the pharmacist, also mentioning her officer father who had been a hero in the previous war. A photograph of each of them had pride of place amongst the flowers. I stared at those portraits of Dammit and the colonel: the same, exactly the same, as appallingly ugly as each other, except that the soldier had a moustache. Three highly qualified rabbis glorified the memory and the courage of this woman who had given her life; then Father Pons took them to see his former collection.

When I married Barbara, Father Pons had an opportunity to go to a real synagogue; he delighted in watching the whole ceremony. Later he often joined us at home to celebrate Yom Kippur, Rosh Hashanah or one of my children's birthdays. But I actually preferred going to Chemlay so that I could go down into the crypt beneath the chapel, a place which still provided comfort with its harmonious disorder. Over the course of thirty years he quite often announced:

'I'm starting a collection.'

Granted, nothing can be likened to the Shoah, and no evil can be compared to another evil, but every time a people on this earth was threatened by other men's madness, Father Pons set about saving things that bore witness to the endangered spirit. Which means he amassed quantities of paraphernalia in his Noah's Ark: there was the Native American collection, the Vietnamese collection, the Tibetan Monk collection . . .

By reading the papers I got to the stage where I could predict when, on my next visit, Father Pons would say:

'I'm starting a collection.'

Rudy and I have remained friends. We contributed to the building of Israel. I gave money, he made it his home. Time and again Father Pons said how happy he was to see Hebrew, that sacred language, resuscitated.

The Yad Vashem Institute in Jerusalem decided to award the title 'Righteous among the Nations' to those who, during the Nazi era and the terror it provoked, incarnated the best of humanity by saving

Jews whose lives were in danger. Father Pons was named as one of the Righteous in December 1983.

He never knew, he had just died. His modesty would probably not have liked the ceremony Rudy and I were planning to arrange; he would probably have protested that he shouldn't be thanked, that he had simply listened to his heart and done his duty. In fact, a celebration like that would have brought most pleasure to us, his children.

This morning Rudy and I went to walk a path through the wood in Israel that bears his name. 'Father Pons Wood' comprises 271 trees representing the 271 children he saved.

There are now young saplings growing at the feet of the older trees.

'Look, Rudy, there are going to be more trees, it won't mean anything any more . . .'

'No, it's right, Joseph. How many children do you have?'

'Four.'

'And grandchildren?'

'Five.'

'When he saved you, Father Pons saved those nine people. Twelve for me. It'll be even more in the next generation. And it'll keep on growing. In a few centuries he will have saved millions of human beings.'

'Like Noah.'

'Do you remember the Bible, you heathen? You surprise me . . .'

Rudy and I are still just as different in every way as we used to be. And we love each other just as much. We can argue vehemently and then give each other a big hug goodnight. Every time I come and see him here, on his farm in what was once Palestine, or when he comes to me in Belgium, we get on to the subject of Israel. Although I support this young nation, I don't approve of all its actions, unlike Rudy who adheres to and justifies the regime's every move, even the most warlike.

'Come off it, Rudy, being in favour of Israel doesn't mean supporting every decision Israel makes. You have to make peace with the Palestinians. They have as much right to live here as you do. It's their territory too. They lived here before Israel was established. The very fact that we have a history of persecution should make us want to say to them the words that we ourselves waited centuries to hear.'

'Yes, but our safety . . .'

'Peace, Rudy, peace, that's what Father Pons taught us to hope for.'

'Don't be naïve, Joseph. The best way to achieve peace is often war.'

'I don't agree. The more hate you build up between the two sides, the harder it will be to find peace.'

Earlier, as we headed back to the olive plantation, we drove past a Palestinian house which had just been destroyed by the tracks of a tank. Things lay scattered in the dust that drifted up into the sky. Two groups of children were fighting violently amongst the rubble.

I asked him to stop the jeep.

'What's this about?'

'Reprisals from our side,' he told me. 'There was a Palestinian suicide bomb yesterday. Three victims. We had to react.'

Without saying anything, I climbed out of the car and walked over to the rubble.

Two rival gangs, Jewish boys and Palestinian boys, were hurling stones at each other. As they kept missing, one of them grabbed a piece of wood, launched himself at the closest adversary and struck him. The retaliation was swift. In a matter of seconds the boys in both gangs were beating each other viciously with broken planks.

I ran over to them, yelling.

Were they frightened? Did they make the most of the diversion to stop fighting? They scattered in opposite directions.

Rudy came over to me slowly, completely relaxed.

I leaned forward and saw some things left by the children. I picked up a kippah and a kiffeyeh. I put one into my right pocket, the other into my left.

'What are you doing?' Rudy asked.

'I'm starting a collection.'